THE CELLAR BELOW THE CELLAR

THE CELLAR BELOW THE CELLAR

IVY GRIMES

This is a work of fiction. All of the characters, organizations, and events portrayed in this novel are either products of the authors' imaginations or are used fictitiously.

The Cellar Below the Cellar

ISBN 978-1-955765-41-1

Cover art by Jack Hillside

Cover design by Mikio Murakami

Violet Lichen Books, an imprint of Apex Book Company

Visit us online at www.violetlichen.com

First Edition: 2026

Printed in the USA

I

IF THE WORLD HAD CARRIED ON AS IT WAS, I MIGHT HAVE given Pastor Dan a second chance after he showed me his demon collection. He was handsome after all, and I felt safe with him since he was a pastor. Most of the women at church wanted to marry him because marrying a pastor was a quick and relatively easy way to raise their social status in our group of friends. I felt so embarrassed for him, though, about his demon jars.

Like all the pastors, Dan made a good salary, and he'd bought a house in a nice part of town. It had three bedrooms, one of which he'd made into a charming little sanctuary with a stained-glass window and an altar with a padded kneeling rail. Since our church had a contemporary design, more like a movie theater, I figured he wanted some old-time religion.

When he insisted on showing me his basement on our third date, I was nervous. I never like to be underground, and how many good dates have ended in basements? But to show I wasn't afraid, I descended with him.

His basement was all concrete and cobwebs lit by bare

bulbs. He directed me to the far wall, where two heavy wooden bookshelves were stocked with mason jars covered in sleeves of bright construction paper. Weird, he didn't seem like the type of guy who made his own fruit preserves.

"This is something very special, Jane," he assured me, plucking a jar from its shelf and displaying the label for me. The words "Ted Bundy" had been written in black marker on the sunny yellow paper, like it was a first-grade craft project filled with imaginary bumble bees. "Since I got saved, I've taken a special interest in suppressing and upsetting demons, keeping them in jail until the time of wrath comes. This one's special. That is, especially evil. It was once inside Ted Bundy, the serial killer."

"But didn't he die before you were born?" I said, trying to sound confused instead of sarcastic.

"Yes, but this demon had been wandering the earth after his execution, until the day it landed on the rail of my front porch. Can you believe it?"

I hoped it was a practical joke. Youth pastors loved to joke around. But he didn't crack a smile this time.

Pastor Dan was vague on his methods, maybe because he didn't want any competitors, but it seemed that through the power of his connection to God or something, he had subdued and captured the demon that had once been inside Ted Bundy.

He showed me more of the jars, telling me about the different kinds of demons, small ones and large ones, ones that looked like apples and ones that looked like rats. They could appear and disappear, run faster than cars, fly in the air like birds. Once a demon possessed someone, it carried a piece of that person's soul forever after. Like a souvenir.

"But now these little demons are trapped all alone," he said, "and that's how they'll remain until the rapture and final judgment when Jesus throws all evil creatures into a lake of fire. I'll be right there beside him, tossing in the ones I caught. I think he'll be proud, Jane. I really do."

"Do you think you'll live long enough to see the final days?" I asked. "Won't you be raptured or something?"

"Jane, surely God won't deprive me of the great pleasure of throwing these little suckers into the eternal lake of fire to be burned beside their master, the great dragon Satan. God's always been good to me, and I've got to bet he'll keep on with his goodness. He will preserve me as one of His own. A demon-catcher and destroyer."

His eyes were like stones smoothed by a river, so striking that I forgot to ask how he'd transport so many jars to that important fire at the end of time. There were way too many of them for one person to carry. I hoped he didn't expect me to help, because I wouldn't. Not even if I'd loved him all my life.

"Do you really hate these demons, or are you kind of... interested in them?" I said. I'd met too many people who were fascinated by evil. Especially too many men.

He recoiled at my question. I'd managed to shock him.

"I definitely hate them... but I guess I'm also interested in them, the way you'd be interested in a science project. Don't you ever get curious about why terrible things happen, or why bad people are the way they are?"

I agreed with him to be polite, but I wasn't sure. I didn't like to think about evil. I was raised by my Grandma to believe in the power of thoughts. She used that power, but it seemed better to me to avoid it.

I pretended to have a good, normal time for the rest of the night while we ate pizza and watched a movie about cartoon penguins rescuing a seal, but the next morning I texted him: “I’m afraid that we aren’t right for each other. I’m sorry!”

He replied: “I got the same message from God. God is good! ;) Let’s be friends.”

Two days later, when I was telling Melissa and Alison at our Sunday small group what happened, I found out that he always reveals the demon jars to women on third dates. Unlike me, they were fine with the demons. What bothered them was his past as a dancer for bachelorette parties. That was his other third-date revelation. I didn't mind that, but it made some women feel uncomfortable given the church’s teachings about the importance of purity, especially for future wives. “Purity” was too esoteric for me, like a fairy in a fairy tale. I was glad to know he could make a living if his pastor gig ever fell through.

The following Friday night, he was off on another first date with Tiffany Belle who headed up the greeting ministry, and I was having dinner with Grandma in her little house in the middle of the woods. I ended up telling her everything that had happened with Pastor Dan, even though I didn’t want to.

Grandma’s most prominent sign of age was that her brow had grown heavier and heavier, putting pressure on her hooded eyes, so that over the years she’d lost the ability to look surprised. Her heavy lids made her seem both world-exhausted and canny, though her face was otherwise relatively unmapped.

In spite of everything, I felt surprisingly jealous of Tiffany Belle and so desperate about my dating life that I started wondering if I could get old Pastor Dan back. Maybe I could live with demon jars in my basement. I could tell him that God had a change of heart about us. Grandma kept me honest, though. She was the only person I knew who made fun of my terrible decisions to my face.

"You keep trying to escape who you are," Grandma said. "You think you can put on and take off masks all the time without changing the face underneath. It's a dangerous game."

"It's not like that exactly," I said. "What I'm doing is putting on masks to see which one feels right. Then my face underneath the mask will know how to go."

Grandma listened, though I could see she didn't understand. She didn't seem to remember what it was like to need people.

"What is it you want from the world?" she said. "What are you chasing after?"

"Does that even matter? Didn't Jesus give to the world instead of taking?"

Grandma hadn't been inside a church for years, but she kept up a knowledge of such things. "You aren't Jesus," she told me.

"I never said I was! But I'm supposed to try, right?"

"I bet Jesus wouldn't waste time with Pastor Dan like you just did."

"He's supposed to love all of us. That must mean wasting time with everyone."

She shook her head. "That's the thing I never understood about him."

I didn't try to proselytize. I'd learned to leave her to her own theology, a muesli of beatitudes, one-liners, intuition, and ancestral paganism.

She sprang to her feet—one flesh and one plastic—to put foil over her casserole dish of roasted sausages, potatoes, and apples. She wouldn't tell me how she lost her other leg, but I'd never seen any old pictures of her where she had both legs. Maybe she'd always been missing one. Her prosthetic had improved in quality over the years, but even when it was blocky and creaky in my earliest days, she was faster than me or Mom. As far back as I could remember, Grandma never got tired.

Outside, a bad storm had swept up, and since she worried about me driving the winding forest roads with poor visibility, I agreed to stay overnight in her guest room. As far as I knew, I was the only guest she ever had.

"It would be cheaper for you to live here and be done with it," she told me, just like she always did.

"It'd take me half an hour to drive to the library every day if I moved here. I can walk to work in ten minutes from my apartment."

"And you think you've got to find a husband, too, don't you? You think you can't do that out here."

"I don't make the rules."

"I do," she said. "You could make them too if you were more like me."

Poor Grandma. She couldn't help that she was a narcissist. Life had shaped her into one, just like it had shaped me into a dutiful and obedient woman, following men right into their basements.

My friend Mallory had organized a brunch party the next day, so I set my phone alarm for 7:30. That would give me time to get home, put on makeup and curl my hair, and pick up pastries to bring along.

As it turned out, I'd never hear that phone alarm again. In the middle of the night, I was disturbed from sleep by a strange green light glowing through my blinds and then a horrible sound, like the biggest cork in the world being popped from the tiniest hole, followed by a quiet crackling, like someone crumpling papers.

Doomsday, I thought. If my church friends were right about the rapture, it looked like Christ was abandoning me with the sinners, because I was still lying in bed and not rising up anywhere.

"Why me?" I said. "Why not me?"

I stumbled to the window and pulled up the blinds. Curved layers of neon green with streaks of red and white lit the sky.

Maybe I was hallucinating. I unplugged my phone from its charger and tried to wake it up to see if anyone else was talking about this, but it was dead. Had there been some kind of power surge? I stood beside my bed, pushing the power button again and again, hoping to force it back to life.

While I was engaged in this fruitless activity, my door creaked open to reveal a ghostly face in the dark hallway, and I screamed.

It was just Grandma; her face appeared unfamiliar in the eerie green light from the window. She looked rather serene, given that the world was ending. She shushed me and motioned for me to follow her.

"I assumed that woke you up," she said.

She led me outside, where it might as well have been daylight. The night had disappeared.

I'd seen pictures of the aurora borealis so I knew what the strange colors in the sky were, but it made no sense to me. We were too far south, and it was far too bright. The light gave Grandma's face a horrible glow, making her look almost demonic.

The night was filled with the sound of crackling cricket legs and rustling pines, which gave my heart an awful surge of adrenaline. I was an early-to-bed, early-to-rise sort of person, not at all fond of late parties or moonlit vigils, not to mention skies the color of poisonous bugs. My blood seemed to freeze inside me. I tried to ignore the kaleidoscope of color, like God's green lava lamp undulating over me. Surely it was a terrible omen.

"I don't like it. Can we go back inside?" I asked.

"What? Look at those beautiful lights in the sky. People travel all over the world to see these. I've done it myself."

As far as I knew, Grandma had never traveled anywhere north of Ohio, but it was no use arguing with her about her past. She always pointed out how little of her life I'd witnessed.

"Grandma, you're acting like this is normal."

"Not at all. I'm almost certain we've never seen anything like this before. It's even bigger than the Carrington Event."

"The what?"

"A geomagnetic storm in the 1850s. This is just like my friend Bill told me it would be. He goes on and on about disasters, and the way he talked about solar storms, I almost looked forward to experiencing one."

"Because of the auroras?"

"Yes, and, to be honest, I wondered if we'd get a break from electricity—and from modern society."

"I'm sure the power will come back on soon."

She laughed. "After a storm this strong? Don't you see how bright it is out here? I'm almost certain we'll lose some comforts we've gotten used to."

"Where does Bill live? Maybe he'll know what to do." I'd met some of her remote friends and neighbors, but there weren't many around. She'd always wanted to live off by herself.

"No, Jane, my friend Bill... he died from a heart attack last year. It's a shame, he'd have loved to have seen this." Her eyes twinkled with interest. It disgusted me. Why would she relish a disaster?

"He'd want to see a horrible glowing sky that looks like aliens have bled all over it?" I wanted to act calm like her, but my hands were shaking, and I was sweating through my pajamas.

"Just the beauty of it. Bill is...*was* a simple man, a prepper. He always said we are too dependent on technology and electricity, and he gave some of his supplies, but I wish I'd listened and prepared more. I guess I got complacent about the whole thing."

"When do you think everything turns back on again?"

"I don't know. Based on that sound and the brightness of the auroras, I'd say this is bad. But I'm no scientist."

"Was Bill a scientist?"

She laughed so hard she couldn't answer. I wondered if she was becoming hysterical.

"This doesn't make any sense," I said. "No one warned us we were in any kind of trouble."

"Trouble comes like a thief in the night," she said, suddenly looking so much younger to me in the aurora-light.

GRANDMA WAS ALREADY UP and busying herself when I woke to the gray morning light pressing on the windows. Could I still see the faintness of the green light behind the gray? Or was that just my imagination.

Tall oaks and pines reached above the roofline, keeping the house in shade all summer, but I raised the blinds to let in as much morning light as I could.

The first thing Grandma did when I entered the kitchen was to say good morning and remind me to stay calm, because she had some news. "I've checked all the battery-powered devices in the house, and none of them work anymore. The electromagnetic storm has destroyed them all."

She paused to let it all sink in, but I didn't want it to. Without batteries, we had nothing. How would I use my phone?

"Tap into those spiritual resources of yours," she said, "and remember that life is more than light, more than power."

"You can't mean all this," I said.

"You should go and check if your car still works," she said..

I grabbed my keys and headed outside to check my ten-year-old Honda Civic, parked out in the gravel driveway. I'd always loved that car, and it had never failed me.

I got in and sat behind the steering wheel for a minute, trying to calm my breathing, praying out loud that God would save my car, that things weren't as bad as Grandma said. I put the key in the ignition, closed my eyes, and turned it. Nothing.

I turned it again. And again. Nothing, not even a small growl from a dying engine. The battery was dead, pure dead.

And with no phone to use, no radio, no television, there was no way to reach my friends or even check the news. My heart raced, and I wanted to cry. What if something very bad had happened in the city?

I looked up and saw Grandma waving at me to come back inside. I ran all the way from the car to the door like I was dashing through a horrible thunderstorm. It seemed like nothing was safe.

She handed me a candle and told me to follow her downstairs to the basement, so she could show me the supplies Bill had left her. I didn't remember her ever mentioning Bill to me before last night, though I tried not to listen to her gossip. This was the first time any of it had been useful to me.

I tried to ignore the flutters of fear. Usually when

Grandma asked me to go down to the basement, I refused. I knew she was hiding more than cans of corn down there. But this time, my interest in her survival supplies outweighed my distrust of the place.

She led me down into the darkness, where she had shelves of flour, sugar, oil, canned vegetables, tuna, bags of candy, bottles of vitamins, all kinds of stuff. Macaroni and cheese boxes. Evaporated milk. It looked like enough to last a lifetime, though maybe it was only a month's worth; I'd never planned out a lifetime of meals.

She had plenty of jugs of water down there too, and she showed me where she kept the tablets to purify our creek water, and a couple of weird little filtering contraptions. We had a creek outside the house, which I assumed was filled with mosquito eggs and animal dung. I'd never considered drinking from it.

"The piped supply of water to our community should last a few days at least, whatever was treated before the power shut off, so we'll need to fill all our empty containers with it," Grandma said. "I bet our neighbors don't know how bad things could be, so we'll have to warn them. But let's keep the extent of our supplies to ourselves for now. That's what Bill told me to do if the time ever came. He said people could get desperate. We'll have to be careful."

"Everything is going to be okay, though, right?" I felt like a child asking such a question. "I mean, sooner or later they'll figure it out and fix the power."

"It depends on how widespread this is. But we always have to prepare for the worst. What we need to do now is check on the neighbors.

I felt the way I'd felt after my mom died when I was a kid, like I was sleepwalking. I nodded and said I'd do whatever Grandma told me to do. Crises made me compliant.

Outside, it was like an ordinary day. Sunlight fell on Grandma's face, making her look older than I remembered, and also livelier. Her little eyes shone with mischief in the midst of her lined face. I'd always hoped to age like her, but lately I only saw her at night. Some things were different during the day, in that kind of light.

As we walked the quarter of a mile to the nearest neighbor, we heard a puffing, mechanical sound in the distance. Soon we caught sight of an old pickup truck chugging down the otherwise empty street towards us.

I waved down the truck, thinking for a minute we were safe again, that the world was still working.

An old man stuck his head and his cigarette out of the driver's window. His truck bed was loaded up with cardboard boxes and covered with a blue tarp.

"You ladies all right?" he rasped out.

Grandma stepped in front of me. "We're doing as well as can be expected," she said.

"What's going on out there? What's happened?" I said, my voice cracking.

"Oh, don't worry, sweetheart," he said. "That solar storm has messed up the power grid is all, but it's nothing we couldn't see coming—well, some of us could see it, maybe."

"How could this happen?" I said. "How could our government not have prepared for it! No offense to scientists, but if you were both worried about this happening, why weren't they?"

He and Grandma smiled at each other like they were in on the same joke.

"I used to trust the government when I was young," he said. "Nothing to feel foolish about, unless you're still doing it when you're old like me."

"You're lucky you have this old thing to drive," Grandma said.

"Lot of fancy new ones are just stopped dead on the roads out there...it's a real mess. If you want, you ladies can ride along with me. I can make some space for you."

He must have taken a liking to Grandma. He was regarding her with raised eyebrows.

"I'm driving out to my brother's place in Jerman City," he said, "just about twenty miles up the road. He's been preparing for the end of time for so long, he's got loads of supplies. I always thought I might get raptured, but then again I was always sort of a rascal, so it makes sense I got left behind."

"Thanks for the offer, but we need to stay right here," Grandma said. "We have to tend to our neighbors. You be careful, now. Good luck out there!"

He gave us a generous grin and tossed his spent cigarette out the window, away from our feet, and he was on his way.

"It's a nightmare," I said. "It must be a nightmare."

"I've been through lots of bad times," Grandma said. "They get easier as the years go by, and we're better off than most."

I didn't know what to say to that. At least we were on a mission, though. I'd met most of Grandma's neighbors a time or two, when she'd brought me along on visits. They were vulnerable people for the most part, elderly or with kids. The closest neighbors, a woman in her forties named Stephanie and her two sons, lived in a manufactured home.

When we arrived, Andrew and Charles were hopping around the front yard, playing with sticks as if they were swords. They were almost teenagers, and I wasn't sure what age you grew out of playing swords, but I figured the end of the world might cause you to regress. They chattered excitedly about what had happened, while Stephanie complained about the power outage. Grandma pried to see how prepared they were. Not very, it seemed, which made her much less cheerful and friendly than she might have been.

"We must be ready for disasters," she said, which seemed unfair since she wouldn't have been ready either, except for the coincidence of knowing this Bill person. "Don't forget to eat all the food in the fridge today, all the stuff that'll go bad. Save the freezer food for tomorrow. The pipes will still bring us clean water for now, but they might not for long, so fill up everything you can with water today. We'll stop by again tomorrow morning."

With Grandma's advice distributed, we marched on up the little road (with everything sparkling in the sun like all was well) to the Ospreys, an elderly couple I'd only met in passing.

Like Grandma, they didn't seem too worried. They bragged about their huge garden in their backyard that could feed ten people.

"You're the most industrious empty nesters I know," Grandma said, which made the Ospreys flinch for some reason. Maybe they wished their grown children were back at home. "But be extra careful about water. Fill up every spare cup and jar you have from your tap. Fill the tub, too."

"That's a good idea," Mr. Osprey said. "We have the creek to drink from too."

"You'll need to filter it, or you'll get sick."

"We don't have any way to do that, I'm afraid."

"I brought some extra contraptions." Grandma pulled one out of her bag and showed them how to use it. They got the hang of it quickly and seemed grateful.

The last stop on our tour was the Bundren family. Jeremiah and Rachel were in their thirties like me, and I'd met them while walking with Grandma before, but I'd never connected with them. It wasn't just the difference in our everyday lives; there was a veil of silence over them, and I simply didn't understand them.

Their three children were friendly enough though, introducing themselves by name and age. There was seven-year-old Ananias, five-year-old Mary, and three-year-old Job. They seemed excited about the oddness of what had happened, just as Stephanie's children had.

Grandma's words of wisdom didn't seem to mean much to the Bundren parents, but they let her in to set up one of her filtration systems on their kitchen counter. She showed them how to use it in excruciating detail, but they barely paid attention. Grandma was oblivious to their lack of interest. She was so obsessed with clean water, she thought everyone must be too.

"The tap water looks fine," Jeremiah said at the end of her demonstration.

"It is right now, but without power, the water company can't keep it clean for long."

"It tastes fine too," Rachel said. Her voice was puny, like she hadn't eaten for a week, and she was wearing a cardigan in spite of the heat. I wondered if she wasn't feeling well, but I didn't dare ask.

Grandma opened her eyes wide, like she always did right before she scolded me, and I ducked into the living room to get away from the conflict. But instead of fussing at them, she began telling them a story I'd heard tons of times about how her father had died too young from drinking unwholesome river water. She told them it happened while he was camping in France, but the details of the story seemed to change every time.

While I waited for her to finish converting the Bundrens,

I looked out the window and watched the children filling up a kiddie pool to play in the backyard. It was so strange to think of having to ration our water.

After she'd repeated her filtering demonstration once more, we were getting hungry and headed home to plunder our own fridge.

We ate the remaining cheese and yogurt and drank milk until our stomachs hurt.

"It'll be okay, won't it, Grandma?" I said. I must have sounded quite pathetic to her.

"It'll be okay," she said

The auroras were just as bright that night, but I had no one to discuss their strangeness with, since Grandma had already accepted them as part of our new natural landscape. With the slightest longing, I thought about Dan. If he'd come to visit Grandma and been stuck here too, he'd have been good company—if I could separate him from his imagination, that is. At least he could have carried heavy things and cut wood for fires. If only he was into canning food instead of jarring demons.

I must have had a premonition, because the first activity Granda recruited me to help with the next day was slicing vegetables and mixing up concoctions.

"Had a bunch of extra cucumbers and squash," she said. "Pickling what's left to make it last. And I have a fantastic idea for what we'll do with the rest of the day!"

I quickly learned that preserving food wasn't much fun. I should have found her comforting then, my old Grandma facing the practical troubles of the world in her quilted robe, making sure each morsel of vegetable would be preserved. Instead, I felt a pit of doom open and expand inside my stomach. I hoped I never had to eat these apocalyptic pickles.

"Are you all right?" she asked me. Something in her tone

and the gleam of fire in her light-blue eyes made it seem like an accusation rather than concern.

"I'm fine!" I said, and after a youth filled with tragedy, I was an expert at pretending to be fine. I'd behaved very well the day before, and no one but Grandma would have suspected I was covering for something. Dan would never have guessed. On that third date when he showed me his demons, he'd complimented my calmness, calling it a gift from God.

"You don't seem fine," Grandma said. "Jane, honey, someday you're going to have to tell yourself the truth about things. When you do that, you'll find resources you didn't know you had."

"I try to be honest, Grandma. I try very hard." I tried to keep the whine out of my voice. She'd known me to be petulant before, of course, because she'd raised me since I was seven years old.

"I know you do. I can also tell you aren't excited about our preparations. But see, an hour of preparation can mean avoiding weeks of cleaning up a mess. There's a time to sew and a time to rip the stitches. A little waste is to be expected, but a lot of waste is a sin."

"What time is it now? Time to sew or time to rip?" I felt angry at her, though I didn't know why. It just didn't seem like the right time to give me advice. I wanted comfort, a hot cup of tea instead of a pickle.

She returned her attention to cutting vegetables. "Right now it is time to be brave, and I don't just mean putting on a happy face. Let yourself freeze right through the core, down into your toes. Freeze yourself to the soil. You know?"

"You mean I should be hard?"

"I mean more than that. I mean, it's time to join up with the earth around you. I've always told you, Jane, that you're more like me than you realize. And if you don't follow in my footsteps, who will?"

"Do you need help with the cucumbers?" I knew I'd never understand her, so I tried to focus on something practical I could do.

She shrugged and stepped aside, but I could tell it wasn't what she wanted. I helped anyway. My arms felt numb, asleep. It was better to give them something to do.

"We have a lot to do this morning," she said, "because today we'll have a big feast to eat up all the cold food before it goes bad."

"I see."

"It's like Mardi Gras. Using up the good stuff to party until we're sick and glad of some deprivation."

I nodded. I was willing to fast or feast, whatever she said. I just wanted to feel sane so I could deal with what was happening. I had to muster all my courage for that sanity.

Something seemed to move below our feet, and a sound like gears screeching reached my ears from deep in the ground. I'd heard that sound at Grandma's house before. I ignored it. I tried to cut in perfectly straight lines. "Will you invite the neighbors to the feast?"

"Of course. We need to form bonds for survival." She jutted her jaw forward like a posing soldier. "They might not be the best team, but they're what we have. Two ignorant families and a pair of old manipulators."

"Sounds good," I said, barely hearing her as I tried to push away any unsettling thoughts. I knew that strong-jawed look of hers rather well. It usually came out in winter. For the time being, we were still in the green part of the year, though we were already nearing the end of summer.

"Someday you'll have to go downstairs and then downstairs," she whispered, and I shut my eyes hard. I knew what she meant. She'd told me about it before: the cellar below the cellar. Maybe I'd been there in dreams, but I refused to step foot in that place in real life.

"Please don't. Not now," I said. The cellar below the cellar was probably just a lie anyway, just an old woman's spinning.

When I opened my eyes, she was back to normal, jolly, bright-eyed. Busying herself. She spoke only of plans for the party as we cut up hunks of beef she'd defrosted to make stew over an outdoor fire.

2

WHEN DAYLIGHT ARRIVED, I SET UP A COUPLE OF CARD tables in the yard for twelve guests and set out our cloth napkins, our best china, and some old silver goblets. Then Grandma sent me off alone to invite the neighbors to the feast while she prepared the appetizers and desserts with the remnants from the freezer. I was to ask everyone to bring a dish to share from their perishable supplies.

I took the same route that Grandma led me down the day before. Andrew and Charles were in the yard again, running around on the field of another invisible battle, while Stephanie sat in a rusting lawn chair, staring solemnly at the grass. She reached out her hand when I approached, and I took it with some confusion. She was acting like I was visiting her at the hospital.

"Grandma would like to invite you to a feast today, so we can all gather and eat our perishable food before it goes bad," I told her, trying to make it sound like more fun than it would really be.

She perked up right away. "What a wonderful idea! I just

love your Grandma. Her strength gives me some strength. I have a key lime pie in the freezer I can bring!"

I had to admit that being the bearer of the invitation made me feel festive, and Stephanie's excitement about the little holiday feast was contagious.

Next, I invited the elderly couple, Mr. and Mrs. Osprey.

"I haven't been to your Grandma's house in a long time," Mrs. Osprey said, squinting her eyes in a meaningful way, but I didn't know how to interpret it. I didn't know they'd ever been to Grandma's house, but of course, she had a life when I wasn't there.

I suggested they bring some vegetables from their garden too, and I moved along.

The last set of neighbors, Jeremiah and Rachel, were outside gathering firewood, and their kids were playing around with hula hoops and water guns like everything was normal. I invited them to the feast, and Rachel gave me a shy smile, but Jeremiah was stony, even when offering up his technically non-ice-cream freezer treat.

As I took my leave, he followed me back to the road.

"Your grandmother is a strange woman," he said.

"Thank you?" I tried to embody her, to be both sweet and sarcastic like she could be.

"In a way, I wonder if this whole thing was her fault."

"This is a pretty big disaster for one little old woman. She can't control the sun." I'd always assumed her neighbors were eccentric since they lived so remotely, and I was almost glad to be proven correct about something.

"I know," he said. "But I get the feeling you don't know what she's capable of. Besides, this is a bigger disaster than you know. My old CB radio worked until I accidentally broke it, and I know that America is finished. Everything we know of and love about our country has collapsed. More than that, too."

My heart fluttered. "There's no more... America? What does that even mean?"

"He's just worried," Rachel said, coming over and patting him on the shoulder. "He's listening to that radio too much."

"It's my heavy load. Not for women to know. I haven't even told my wife what's really going on, and I won't tell you."

He really wouldn't tell me any more than that. Just enough to terrify me without any details to analyze. "You don't have to come to our party if you don't feel like it," I said, hoping he wouldn't, but he insisted they would be there with their so-called ice cream.

When I returned home, Grandma told me to shower and wash my hair, because soon the stored water would be gone, and we'd have to bathe another way. I told her what Jeremiah said, but she waved it off.

"Most people don't know anything, and neither does he. Besides, if America is over, then something new will come in its place. Don't worry, hon. There's nothing you can do about it anyway."

She was right, there was nothing I could do, so I tried my best to forget my concerns. I was hot from my journey and the house was stuffy with no AC, so I didn't mind the cold shower. I emerged feeling new and normal and put on an old out-of-style dress I'd worn back in high school and left at Grandma's house. What did style matter anymore?

But I shushed that hopeless thought and pushed it away. I still needed to believe in things like style if I was going to stay calm. I had to ignore the looming bad news. The shock of the dark reality might kill me, and I couldn't die yet. I had to summon my inner strength, which Grandma always said was my birthright from her side of the family. I had to do it for the kids in the neighborhood, so they wouldn't be too scared. Childhood fears were much more terrible than adult fears, because children hadn't learned to ignore their dreams. I shook off the bad thoughts and went into the kitchen to help Grandma with the feast.

"This is a day to remember," Grandma said. "A feast day the likes of which we won't see again."

"Please don't say that," I said.

"We'll have better ones later! We just won't have some of these delicacies again. We'll have to invent better ones."

Grandma wanted us to enjoy the arrival of the auroras after sunset, so I found some white tablecloths and cut magnolias and roses to decorate the tables. Soon, our backyard seemed ready for the Mad Hatter and the Dormouse. I hadn't even known she owned so many party supplies. Who knows what someone might store away, though, if they have a cellar below their cellar. I didn't want to think about that, so I busied myself with preparations instead. I pulled out a box of my old toys – soccer balls, a badminton set, a few old action figures – for the kids to play with.

As soon as everyone arrived, the older kids, Andrew, Charles, and Ananias, began kicking around a soccer ball, while Mary and Job played with my old action figures (which were pink to indicate girlhood, but Job was too young to know). I kept an eye on them while the adults went inside to add their meager contributions to our feast.

Soon it was time to eat, and we loaded our plates with stew and fire-baked cobblers and pigs-in-a-blanket and bacon and American cheese – everything that would go bad soon. I couldn't believe how much the kids ate. Grandma gave everyone a lukewarm beer from the stash in her fridge, including the two oldest boys who were still far too young for alcohol. When I looked at her funny, she whispered, "Where's John Law now?"

The night before, she'd told me that the neighbors didn't understand how bad things were but that I shouldn't scare them. We all had to stay strong for the kids.

The only way I could stay strong was not to ask too many questions. I'd asked too much about Mom when I was too young, about how she died and all the details. I'd begged until Grandma told me more, and then I'd wished I hadn't asked. Mom had gotten quite ill and taken her own life. That was the only other time I had ever felt like it was the end of the world.

The kids ate fast and went back to playing, and I found myself moving between them and the adults, who were making awkward small talk. They'd exhausted the topic of the auroras, which they all agreed were spectacular but couldn't find anything else to say about. I wondered when we'd get tired of seeing that brilliant sky.

Mrs. Osprey asked me how old I was, and I felt myself blush, though I didn't know why.

"Thirty-three," I said.

"And you still live with your grandmother?" Mrs. Osprey kept at me, smirking. It seemed she was trying to embarrass me, but I wondered what on earth she could have against me.

"Jane lived in town," Grandma said, methodically slicing her food into bite-sized pieces. "In an apartment with roommates."

"Lived in town, I see. And now...?" Mr. Osprey said, smiling in a way I didn't like. There was a flirtatious gleam in his eye.

"I still live there. Once things settle down, or are resolved, I'll..." I didn't finish my sentence, because Grandma shook her head. That was exactly the subject she didn't want us discussing that day. The future.

Stephanie seemed to feel sorry for me and helped change the subject. "It's lucky the kids are out of school for the summer," she said. "If we were in the middle of the schoolyear, the school would have to shut down for who knows how long."

That topic of conversation didn't catch on either. The only other people there with young kids were Jeremiah and Rachel, and they were both pretty quiet. They looked so sad, but Grandma had outlawed sad talk. They didn't eat much compared to the rest of us, either, just some potato chips and grapes.

"How old are Andrew and Charles?" I asked Stephanie, unable to think of a question that wasn't about age, and I wasn't bold enough to ask Mr. and Mrs. Osprey their ages.

"Charles is fourteen, and Andrew just turned twelve. They're a real handful. I think this disaster has made them happier than anything ever has. Are you sure none of you have any kind of radio that works? Some kinds of radios work even if the power's off."

I looked over at Jeremiah to see if he'd pipe up, but he was pretending to be fixated by something on the ground. Afraid of Grandma, probably.

"No," Grandma said sharply. "I told you, today is a feast day. We aren't going to talk about our problems."

"Sorry." Stephanie looked at her lap. I knew how she felt.

"If it wasn't for Bill, we wouldn't have anything," I said, rushing to fill in the awkward silence.

"Who's Bill?" everyone said at once, and Grandma glared at me. I seemed to remember she told me not to mention him.

"He used to live nearby," she said, "past Maple and down

the little dirt road to the back of The Food Fellow. He gave us a few supplies, nothing big. Some of the stuff you're enjoying today is because of him. He's dead now, sadly, of complications from diabetes."

Everyone groaned, and that started up a real conversation since each of them knew someone with diabetes. Or had known someone.

"If things keep up, I guess we won't have to be careful what we eat anymore when it comes to our health," Mrs. Osprey said. "Won't have many options to choose from."

Grandma gave her a death stare, but Mrs. Osprey stared right back.

"We have tomatoes and peppers and other things growing out back," Mr. Osprey said. "We're happy to share as they ripen, but we'll need some help tending to the garden, though, especially now that chores take so much more time. If only all our sons had been home when this thing happened."

"We have blackberry bushes," Stephanie said, smiling at us, "and the berries are almost ready for picking. We'll bring some for everyone pretty soon."

If everyone could keep their head and share what they had, I could see a path towards a kind of community I'd never known.. I'd bet anything that Grandma wasn't going to tell anyone about everything she had stored in the cellar though, much less in the cellar below the cellar. I was the only one she wanted to entrust with that awful knowledge, but even the thought of it made my stomach twist.

"We can make some blackberry preserves to put aside in jars," Grandma said. "I'll show you how."

"Oh, no, I'm too lazy for that, I'm afraid," Stephanie said.

I smiled, but Grandma didn't. I wished I had the guts to

reject Grandma's instruction sometimes. Maybe Stephanie would teach me a thing or two.

Our moods improved as we stuffed ourselves, and soon we reached a tipping point of tiredness. The kids played while the parents napped in the shade, and Mr. and Mrs. Osprey chatted with Grandma about how people used to be more self-reliant in their day. I was grateful when Mary, the Bundren's five-year-old, pulled me away from the adults to play action figures with her.

As the sun went down, the auroras returned to us, silent alarms in the sky. I tried not to look up at the weird wormy colors, but Mary loved them and kept clapping and pointing at the twisting shades of blue and green. The light they cast on her face made her look like a little alien.

Eventually, it was time for the action figures to sleep, and Mary informed me that they were going camping, so we built them tents out of wide leaves.

"It's like we're camping inside our houses now," she said.

"It's true," I told her. "No electricity. No AC. No fridge. It's not easy."

"It's fun!"

"I'm glad your family is having fun."

"I am, but Mom and Dad aren't. They're scared."

"Of what?"

She shrugged, and I wondered if she really didn't know or was just feeling contrary because I'd taken an interest in what she had to say.

"But they don't like your grandma. My mom says she might be smart, but she's rude."

"Grandma is smart," I said, for her sake as well as mine. I didn't like them talking about Grandma behind her back, even if what they said was true. "She's solved a lot of problems for me already."

"Her house is scary, though."

"Why?"

"Something's in there," she said.

Her words unnerved me, but I'd spent enough time around kids at the library to know they said weird things all the time.

"There's nothing scary in there," I said, lying like adults always did. "Everything here is safe."

Mary clammed up after that, and I didn't blame her. I'd always hated it when adults lied to me. Now I knew they had no choice.

When the Bundrens left, carrying the three-year-old down the green-lit driveway while Mary and Ananias tagged along behind, they paused to wave goodbye and tried to give us a smile. I felt a pang of sadness for them. They all looked so young and vulnerable, parents and kids alike.

Stephanie and her sons left too, but the Ospreys lingered behind for some reason. It turned out they had a request.

"Our garden is really going to help the community," Mrs. Osprey said, "but we're getting old, and we both have arthritis. We'd get a much better harvest from it if we had an extra hand." She stared right at me.

"Oh, I'm sure Jane would be delighted to help!" Grandma said before I could protest. "She loves to get her hands dirty."

I agreed to start coming by to help with the garden, but I wasn't looking forward to seeing them again, which was a shame since there were so few people living out here.

That night, I lay in bed, reading by the green light of the aurora when an even brighter wave of light lit up the night. What was wrong with the sun? The sound that followed was familiar to me, the massive snap, the electric crackling.

My heart sank. I'd hoped God would have heard us asking for help, but maybe we'd done something to provoke him.

3

I STAYED IN BED THE ENTIRE NEXT DAY, WHICH WAS Monday, and who cared anymore? In spite of my absent alarm, I had woken up early thinking it was time to go to the library. I had to remind myself there weren't any phones that worked, and the power was still out. Grandma kept telling me I should be grateful I happened to be at her place in the woods when we lost power. It might have been more fun with my roommates, or maybe we'd fight all the time about our small pile of supplies.

Grandma refused to talk about the second solar storm other than acknowledge it had happened, but she wouldn't indulge my worrying about it. She must have felt sorry for me when I stayed in bed all morning, though, because she brought me orange slices and bread with butter and coffee. She said we had to eat things up in the order that they'd go bad.

"What will we do when it all runs out?" I said, propped up in bed, listlessly sucking on orange slices. "Will the National Guard come and help us?"

"Don't worry, all will be well. That's not for you to trouble yourself about. You need to keep up your mental strength, and to do that, you'll need a project to work on."

It was true I withered when I didn't have something to busy my mind. It had happened to me before, as Grandma knew. I'd learned to stay busy with church and volunteer work and my job at the library, but those had all receded like a low tide, and I was stranded. The truth was, though Grandma would never admit it, I had a tendency towards depression like my mother, even in the best of times.

"Today you can rest, but tomorrow you'll go over to the Ospreys," she said. "I bet they already have seeds laid up for a fall harvest of pumpkins and squash. That'll help us a great deal. Very nutritious."

I wiped my sticky fingers on the cloth napkin she'd placed so nicely between my plate and tray, and I decided to be honest with her. "Who cares about fall vegetables, Grandma? I know you don't want to hear it, but I don't really care about anything right now. Not the neighbors. Not running pointless errands. Don't you get how bad things are? I don't think I can face it."

She laughed at me. "Of course, hon, but you have to carry on. For my sake. For the Ospreys. For the five kids and three parents. You can't just hide in your little hole."

I began to cry, which always made Grandma withdraw from me. She took away the breakfast things and left me to recover. I lay in bed and stared at the bits of blue sky between the blinds. At some point, I returned to sleep and dreamed about moving cardboard boxes full of snow from Grandma's kitchen to the living room. Someone needed them for something, but no one would tell me why. I woke up wondering why I couldn't even rest in my dreams. That convinced me that Grandma was right, that I needed something to keep me busy in real life. With any luck, I'd be so tired at the end of the day, I'd have a dreamless sleep.

The next day, she dressed me in her gardening clothes and put a straw hat on my head and sent me over to the Ospreys. They were my least favorite people so far, but they were the only ones with the garden.

When I knocked on the door, they were nicer to me than before.

"Your grandmother told us you were feeling a bit down," Mrs. Osprey said.

"Anyone would under these conditions," Mr. Osprey said, "but especially a young person with her whole life ahead of her. If only you'd already gotten a husband."

"We need more men who can work with their hands around here," Mrs. Osprey said. "It's not like we're that old-fashioned. But you see, we have to think practically now."

They had a point. Still, if I could get back to the city and find my friends, I might join up with them instead of Grandma's spread-out community of forest people. Weird people. Lonely people. And yet, I owed Grandma everything, and I couldn't leave her alone.

"Can I ask you one question?" My stomach hurt to go behind Grandma's back to ask, but I could tell she was protecting me from something. "What do you think happened? No one's given me any news, and Grandma won't talk about it. Could people have died?"

The Ospreys looked at each other, opening their mouths and closing them like animals trying to speak our language. "Your grandmother says you worry too much," Mrs. Osprey said at last. "There's nothing you can do about what's out there, so you'd best focus on what you can control."

"But what do you think happened?"

Mr. Osprey cleared his throat. "We don't want to talk

about the worst-case scenarios. We don't have the energy, because we have to take care of things right here. We all promised we wouldn't talk about that."

"I didn't promise."

"Your grandmother promised on your behalf."

"When?"

"At the feast."

"Behind my back!" My voice shook a little. I hated these stupid dramatics, but damn it, she wasn't going to turn me into a little girl again.

"You have to respect our wishes," Mrs. Osprey said. "We've been down some hard paths, and we believe God is always leading us. You're still a child, really, and you haven't seen true darkness yet. I pray you never do."

I gave in and dropped the matter, hoping I could get the children to tell me what their parents were saying. What if I had no friends left in the city? What if the city was lined with the upturned palms of the dead?

Seeing that I was ready to keep the gruesome matters to myself, the Ospreys gave me a trowel and set me out to the cleared part of the garden to plant pumpkin seeds. Just as Grandma had hoped, they were trying to coax a big crop. They rattled off facts about pumpkins, how much summer sun they needed, how much water, how much compost. They said Grandma had begun composting for the sake of their garden, and she would show me how. I took it all in, knowing they'd repeat themselves hundreds of times. There was only so much that could be said about planting, or so I thought at the time.

Once I was done with the garden work, they brought me a glass of lemonade. I felt the grit of the cheap lemonade powder between my teeth, but still, it wasn't bad. I was getting used to lukewarm drinks.

"We're almost out of bottled water, but we're lucky to have the creek," Mr. Osprey said. "Your grandmother has been showing everyone how to filter it."

Since I'd done my duty for the day, he took my empty glass and gave me one green pepper to take to Grandma. I pretended to be pleased with it as my wage for the day, and I tried to put some fake cheer into my goodbye.

I carried the pepper back in both hands so I wouldn't drop it. I wondered if she'd use it in a stew or if she'd savor it raw, eating the fresh strips.

By the time I got home, I'd lost the pepper. It was the strangest thing. I was holding it one moment, and the next my hands were empty. I didn't taste it. I hadn't eaten it myself. I hadn't met anyone along the way. I surely wouldn't have dropped it since I was cradling it in my hands.

I told Grandma about the disappearing pepper when I got home, and she seemed ashamed for my sake. I stood in the dark doorway, my hands shaking, while she sat before a crackling fire with the windows all open, a big pot on a rack boiling away.

"Don't tell anybody else that story, or it'll make you sound stupid," she said

"Maybe I am stupid! I'm confused by everything that's happening." I wanted to cry, but I sensed it would only make her angry at me. It seemed to me that Grandma's very body had changed, that she was growing taller. Still a bit hunched and gray, but sprouting like a child.

"It's fine to be confused," she said. "But don't tell everyone what you're thinking. We have to survive together, and you need to act like you're capable. Otherwise, your weakness will cause weakness in others. It's not just about you, Jane. For the very first time in your life."

My eyes filled with tears, and I felt so ashamed. I was selfish, and now that the world was falling apart, I was no help. I'd always told myself I was a good granddaughter, but I must have been kidding myself.

"So...I was wrong about the pepper?" I said. I wished she'd just tell me I was wrong so I could stop thinking about it. I'd rather be crazy than lose the continuity of the world.

"You were wrong to tell me about the pepper. Better me than anyone else, but I have my own problems at the moment. You must learn to keep your problems to yourself. Did you plant a lot of pumpkin seeds?" She flipped right from scolding to smiling at me.

"It was boring, but whatever." I wiped my eyes with my forearms, still feeling like my hands were dirty. "They told me to bring some compost along tomorrow."

"We'll have a good batch. I'm keeping it in a bin out back. Want me to show you?"

"No," I said. But I followed her anyway and politely listened as she explained our new composting routine.

⚜ 4 ⚜

I WENT TO BED EARLY THAT NIGHT, BUT I DIDN'T SLEEP. I stared at the lights and tried to pretend I was on an expensive trip to Iceland, but it didn't work. For one thing, it was hot in the house without the AC. While I was lying in bed like a slug, I heard a loud knock at the door, which startled me. Who was bothering us at night? Part of me hoped it was the government in some form, coming to bail us out, or at least reassure us that everything would be restored.

Grandma was ahead of me answering the door, where we found Jeremiah on our doorstep, looking pale and sickly as he clutched his lifeless-looking daughter to his chest."

"What's the trouble, Jeremiah?" Grandma said.

"It's little Mary." He had tears in his eyes. "She's gotten worse. A bad fever now like everyone else, and she won't open her eyes anymore. I wanted to bring her before I got too sick."

"I'm glad you had the good sense to bring her, Son."

Grandma directed him to place Mary on the soft couch in

the den. She covered her with blankets and boiled water in the fireplace.

"She just needs my fever tea, and then she needs to sleep a long time. Just like the rest of you."

Without complaint, Mary drank the fever tea (some foul-smelling herb mixture I'd never seen Grandma make before), and she fell asleep in a nest of blankets.

"Why don't you stay, too?" she said to Jeremiah.

Where were we going to put all these people?

"No, ma'am, I certainly can't. I need to get back to Rachel right away. I can't leave her." He started to cry, and his face turned red. I looked away so he wouldn't be embarrassed.

Grandma walked him outside and talked to him for a while, and before long he was gone.

My nerves were bothering me after all that, so I asked Grandma if I could have some of the tea as well.

"Strictly for fever," she said. "But tomorrow I'll make up a batch for nerves."

Without anything else to do, I picked a pretty blue gold-engraved hardcover book called *Lost Horizon* out of Grandma's bookshelf (I was longing, I suppose, for the long rows at the public library) and sat in an armchair near Mary, prepared to be awake for the rest of the night. I must have drifted off, because I was startled awake by the sound of Mary sleep-talking. I looked around for Grandma, but she wasn't around, neither in her bedroom nor right outside the front door. I was getting pretty tired of her volunteering me for jobs I didn't want to do. I'd never taken care of a sick kid before.

"I don't want to." That was one thing Mary said as she clawed at her blankets, her eyes shut.

"Don't want to do what?" I said.

"I don't want to help!"

"Fair enough." I leaned back in my chair. "You don't need to help. Just rest. You're just a little kid."

"Quelle catastrophe," she mumbled. I took French in high school, and I'm pretty sure that's what she said. If she said something in English, which is more likely, she might have said "Quit the camp," or "Quit carrying me."

I answered as if she'd said the word catastrophe, which was how I felt. "I wonder why all these terrible things are happening. Maybe there is no reason."

Mary began to cough, which woke her all the way up. I poured her a glass of water from one of the jugs Grandma had set aside.

"I'm sorry you're sick," I told her.

"I thought I was going to die," she said. "And I wasn't sad about it."

"Well, these are strange times. But you have to keep your strength up, for your sake as well as everyone else's. Think how sad we'd all be if you died."

She looked confused, so I decided she was too young and sick for such morbid talk. I went up the ladder into the attic and got a box of children's books for her, filled with picture books as well as classics like *Little House on the Prairie*.

When I returned to her, though, she was vomiting. It almost made me sick, too. I'd seen a few children vomit at the library, but I never got used to it. It was fundamentally not right, not acceptable. It wasn't that it was unacceptable on the part of the children but on the part of life. It wasn't right for life to reject life that way.

The blankets were ruined, and of course, there was no washing machine for them. I panicked a little and called for Grandma. When she didn't arrive right away, I put all the affected items in the bathtub and cleaned Mary off with wet rags as best I could. I put her in one of my old T-shirts, a red one that said "Church Service Team" that I used to wear when I volunteered to make the coffee before church. Once Mary was relatively clean, I found more blankets for her. Grandma certainly had no shortage of blankets.

"Does your stomach still hurt?" I asked her.

She nodded pitifully. When I touched her forehead, it felt dangerously hot. Maybe it was the force of the fire in the room on a warm summer evening, but it worried me. I'd never known a kid who had died before. I'd had too much fun before, let myself ignore despair, ignore all the ugly stuff that happened to people I didn't know. Now I was in the shadows, so unlucky I'd probably be the one who had to dig her grave. Grandma would probably make me. If it came to that, I figured I'd join her there.

I gave Mary another glass of water and searched the kitchen for something I could pretend was a remedy. Grandma had already emptied the fridge and freezer, and she'd moved the pickles down to the awful cellar, but I refused to go down there without her. She'd taken to hanging herbs in the window to dry, but I only recognized mint and rosemary, which didn't seem particularly healing. Then again, maybe it was worth a try.

I returned and told Mary to eat three dwindling mint leaves, to smush them up well with her teeth. She did as I requested, finished her water, and fell back to sleep. I sat up with her for what felt like hours, alarmed by her condition. Every so often, I felt her forehead and began to worry again. When I looked out the window to search for Grandma, I had to admit it was beautiful outside, with soft bluish lights. I imagined Grandma relishing the beauty of the auroras while she did her weird business, and it made me angry. This was no time to be distracted by beauty.

By the time Grandma returned home, dawn was breaking.

A black knit hat was pulled low over her fuzzy gray hair, and her arms were full of flowers and weeds.

"She's really sick!" I cried out. I'd never been so annoyed with Grandma. Every time I'd ever needed her before, she'd been at home. "Where did you go? You think those plants will cure her?" I ranted a bit about how we were all doomed.

Grandma only laughed at me. "It's not easy to be your age," she said. "You should sleep now. I already went by the Ospreys and said you wouldn't be helping them today. I'll clean up everything."

I wanted to cry, but I found myself running away like I was a kid again, pounding my heels, slamming the door. I felt guilty when I realized I might have woken up Mary, which made me mad all over again. I shouldn't have to feel guilty! I shouldn't have to feel like a prisoner! I wasn't a kid anymore, and Grandma couldn't just boss me around. Sure, I had a day off from my new unwanted job at the Ospreys scratching at the dirt and pulling brittle weeds, but my life wasn't my own anymore.

For a moment, I contemplated risking it all and running all the way back to my apartment. I desperately missed the library.

I was so tired, though. I slept deeply, slept long, like surrendering to a tub of hot water.

When I awoke, it was well past midday. In the mornings, the light flowed through my window and onto my bed like an invitation, but in the afternoons, it kept away. I went to the bathroom for the jug of water, soap, and washcloth that helped me feel almost clean again.

The tub was empty of blankets. Of course, Grandma always did what she promised. I put on an old sundress from high school that was a bit too small for me, wondering what I'd do when I ran out of clothes I kept at Grandma's house. I guessed I'd start to wear her clothes eventually, and they'd be small on me as well. She'd have to let them out for me.

I was shocked to find Mary sitting up and smiling in the living room, still wearing my T-shirt. Eyes bright.

"You slept forever," she said.

"Do you feel better?"

"Yes. I like it better here when it's sunny. I don't like the nighttime here."

All children were scared of the dark, as far as I knew. I'd been scared of it. Helping her get over that fear was a project for her parents. "Do you know when your parents are coming back for you?"

Grandma interrupted us, calling me into the kitchen where she was sitting at her little wooden table in the gray sunlight, reading a book that did not appear to have a title. When I looked closer, I saw it was handwritten, but she closed it and motioned for me to sit down.

"Mary is going to stay with us a while," she said, with a slight tone of impatience, as though I should have known.

"Why? For how long? Do her parents know that?"

"Of course they know!"

"But why?"

"Three kids, small house. They've all come down with a bug. Anything we can do to take a load off their minds will help. Taking care of Mary is the very least we can do, I assure you."

I leaned closer to Grandma and lowered my voice, hoping that Mary (observant as I could tell she was) wasn't listening. "What's the real reason you want her here?"

Grandma smiled. "I'm proud of you," she said at her normal volume. "You're starting to really think about things."

"Is this because I'm not married? You want Mary so you

can feel like you have a granddaughter? I mean, a great-granddaughter?"

This question angered Grandma in a way I hadn't seen in some time. She thumped her hand on the table and pressed her lips together, and though I wanted to run away, I remained perfectly still and focused on the gold embroidery on her book.

"How dare you talk to me like I'm a stupid old woman? I'm the one keeping everyone alive while you act like you're shell-shocked."

"I am shell-shocked," I said, hoping I was capable of standing up for myself. I hadn't lived with Grandma since I was eighteen, had left as soon as I could to have my own space, and suddenly my own space had evaporated. Grandma was all I had.

"Why can't I lie around and be scared, too?" Grandma said.

"You can if you want!"

"And then who would help all these people? Who would keep you alive? And here you think I want to work for other people all the time, that I'd even want a child I can feed and dress up like a doll. Does that sound like me?"

"No," I said. It didn't.

"Then trust me, I have my reasons. If you spent more time thinking and less time dreaming, you'd already know why I want her here."

More riddles from Grandma! She was funny and endearing when I only saw her once a week, but I was getting tired of her obfuscations. Why did she want Mary here if it wasn't because she missed taking care of a little girl? Grandma must have had a plan for her, but I couldn't figure out what it was. Mary had some kind of knowledge of what was going on in the house. She was so little, but she was smart. Smarter than I was at that age by far.

"Why *do* you want her here?"

"I don't want to hear any more about it right now—we have too many practical concerns to take care of. I need to start filtering more water. Nothing's more important than clean water. But we also need to eat something nutritious to keep up our strength. I'll make some biscuits over the fire, but I need you to go down into the basement and get us something for dinner. If you think you can manage that."

Her condescension made me so indignant that I agreed to go to the cellar without any complaint. I took a candle to light the way and tried to pretend I wasn't afraid of the enveloping darkness. It was cool down there, though, a relief from the overheated upstairs. Still, I didn't like to be the only source of light in a room. I quickly scanned the various cans and bottles to find some soup and a jar of preserves.

I felt a short rumble beneath my feet, from the cellar beneath the cellar. I didn't believe in monsters, not even human ones, so why did the thought of what was down there —if anything— make me shiver? Almost every time I visited Grandma, she tried to talk me into going down there. She was always pushing me to do something I didn't want to do, to make me into someone new. She acted like I was made of clay, something for her to fashion. She'd always done that, telling me which friends and career paths were unacceptable, making mean remarks about bands and books I liked that she thought were beneath me. Maybe that was what she kept in the cellar below the cellar, all the things she considered beneath us. Silly pop songs about love. Stupid youth pastors. Internet stars. Jewelry. Tardiness. Laziness, above all else. Maybe the cellar beneath the cellar was filled with idle hands.

It was easier to live in the house this way, feeling like there wasn't any real evil, especially at night when it was so dark without electric lights. I prayed nothing in the house would harm me, Grandma, or our new ward, and I almost forgot why I was down there. I chose two cans of chicken noodle soup and a small jar of fig preserves.

"Good choices," Grandma said when I returned upstairs. She was letting creek water filter through the contraption on the counter while she mixed dough with her bare hands. "Go look after Mary for me. Get her some more nice, clean water and read to her. We have to keep up with her education, after all."

Maybe so, maybe not. Maybe we'd never have lights or school again. Whatever the case, it was more comfortable to do what she said. I picked up *Little House on the Prairie* and read to Mary, who was a nice and inquisitive child. She no longer smelled like sickness.

After I read for a little while, I paused for a minute, and Mary asked me what was wrong.

"This family has such a hard time surviving," I said. "And for what? They didn't even belong here. They weren't from here."

"Where were they from?"

I thought about making something up, but I couldn't lie to the kid. "I don't know. I don't even know where most people in *my* family were from. Only Grandma's side. Her ancestors were missionaries from Switzerland, but they came here later—at the end of the 1800s, I think. They were in some kind of weird old Swiss sect who believed you have to perform certain rites before you die, but most people don't know how to die right. Her family tried to teach them."

I'd only half-listened to Grandma's genealogy lessons over the years, so I couldn't quite remember the details. Only that it seemed like a weird pagan version of Christianity, something the pastors at my church might have called witchery. Still, their beliefs must have been pretty powerful to make them go so far from home just to teach people how to die.

"Jane?" Mary said, interrupting my fruitless pondering. "Why do some people stick around after they die?"

"Why do you ask that?"

She wouldn't look at me. "I don't know."

Maybe she really had seen a ghost. I had no idea how to answer her question. I didn't know anyone who had stuck around after death. I wished I did!

Grandma hurried into the living room to put the cast-iron pan on the fire and said, "Stop talking about morbid things."

I kept reading at Grandma's request, and she listened to me while she cooked the biscuits.

"Some people will do anything for a little adventure." That was her only commentary on the reading.

5

Soon enough, I had to return to the Ospreys. When I arrived, they asked if I enjoyed the green pepper they'd given me. They didn't ask how Mary was doing, or how Grandma or I were doing. All they cared about was that pepper, it seemed. I couldn't think of what else to say, so I told them the truth. I must have forgotten Grandma's warnings.

"It disappeared in my hands on the way. I can't explain it."

They smirked at each other, then hid their smiles when they looked at me. That kind of thing infuriated me. What was so foolish or cute about my blacking out while holding a vegetable?

"Don't worry," Mrs. Osprey said. "These things happen. Life is full of loss. We have plenty more peppers, though. More and more to come, too, with all this work you're doing."

I nodded, too annoyed to speak more and accept any compliments. I followed them outside and did my assigned weeding and watering. I'd always been curious about gardening, but before I'd felt too busy to even put flowers in a planter. So far, I had discovered I hated it. I hated accidentally cutting worms in half with my trowel and watching both pieces wriggle. The weeds that clung hardest to the dirt infuriated me when they refused to be pulled up in one clump. Once I was on the path back to Grandma's, I'd often find ticks and spiders and other ugly things on my arms and legs. I got sweaty in the late June heat, and I couldn't even have a shower when I was done. Grandma said that once a week, we could each take a hot bath with boiled creek water dumped into the tub. It was the kind of bath that sometimes left more dirt on me than it washed away, but it was relaxing. The rest of the time, I had to give myself a spit bath with a gallon jug of distilled water or take some soap right into the creek. Between that and the garden work, I felt dirty all the time.

I did wonder if the garish colors of the auroras had some impact on the vegetables, like if their hues added some extra fertilizer, or maybe a bit of magic. I wouldn't want to eat a tomato that was streaked with those colors. The auroras were beautiful, but too beautiful for everyday life. I tried not to stare at them too often.

After my gardening, the Osprey's asked me "to make up for the time I was gone tending to Mary" by doing some chores in the house. I swept the floors and washed some dishes and quietly despised the Ospreys. Why couldn't Grandma make her own garden so we could be free of them?

They talked to me the whole time I did my indoor chores, telling me about their sons. One lived in Massachusetts, one in Maine, one in Michigan. They all had good jobs and lived in mansions with servants. They seemed to really want me to believe that, and that their sons were surely already finding ways to overcome the debilitations of the Big Trouble, as the Ospreys called it. Grandma called it the Disaster. We hadn't workshopped an official title for it, but if we had, I would have objected to "Big Trouble" since it sounded like the title of a kid's movie. Still, it managed to capture something about how I felt.

Before I was done for the day, another worker arrived: Stephanie's oldest son, Charles. I wanted to ask how his family was doing, but the Ospreys sent him out right away to chop wood for the fire.

"I wonder if everyone would help us like this if we didn't have our garden to repay them with!" Mrs. Osprey said once the kid and her husband were outside with the ax.

"It would probably depend on the strength of your personal connections," I said, unable to stop myself.

"Thank God we don't have to depend on that," she said.

When I left that afternoon, I carried a small basket of produce that I expected would disappear along the way, though I resolved to keep my eyes open. Two tomatoes, two cucumbers, two peppers. It was enough to make a salad, if I made it home with them.

On the way, it occurred to me to take a detour to Stephanie's. Grandma had asked me to keep away from the other neighbors until they got used to things, so that any depressive attitudes would not affect me, but I decided to risk it. I was already pretty depressed.

Stephanie's house was more like a trailer with the wheels removed, and the yard was filled with old toys, a rusty car, and some other junk. While I knocked and waited, knocked and waited, I stared at an octopus-patterned kiddie pool nearby. It looked relatively clean, though the plastic bottom was full of silt. They must have been using it for baths.

No one answered, so I considered giving up and going home. She was out hunting and gathering, maybe. But then Andrew, her twelve-year-old, pulled the door open slightly and looked up at me without saying anything.

"I'm here to see your mom," I said.

"I'll ask her," he said, and his footsteps ran to some hidden corner of the house.

When he returned, he was cautious. "Can you come to her room? It's messy," he warned me.

"Everything's messy now," I said.

He led me inside, which smelled a bit like sour milk, and down the hall to Stephanie's bedroom.

Her bedroom walls were all paneled with fake wood, which made the place feel like a hollow log. One small window was open to let in the languid breeze, but it was still stuffy and hot. Stephanie was lying in the fetal position, curled up with a sheet over her. Her comforter was in a pile on the floor, probably kicked off days before.

I stood there awkwardly holding my small harvest of vegetables.

Stephanie patted the bed, inviting me to sit there, which I did, holding my basket in my lap.

"Are you okay?" I said, no doubt sounding as stupid as I felt.

"I'm not contagious," she said. "I'm just having a hard time with all this."

"Understandable."

"Then you're the only one who understands," Stephanie said. "The Ospreys told me I was an unfit mother. Your grandmother stops by every day to help with things, but I have a feeling she doesn't understand me. She told me that Mary is staying with you two. Jeremiah and Rachel haven't stopped by to see me either, but I guess they caught some bug. It feels like it's been ages since that feast day. That day, it seemed like everything would be okay."

I should have felt close to her then since she was the only person I'd met who was expressing what I thought was an honest or normal emotion in the wake of the Disaster. She smelled terrible, though. I knew I was supposed to hug her or something, but I couldn't overcome my repulsion. The smell of sour milk from the kitchen mixed with the scent of her body odor and something rotting, maybe a dead animal under the window. I kept reminding myself to breathe through my mouth, but I still felt like I was absorbing noxious fumes that way. I tried to convey a sense of camaraderie and understanding in spite of my discomfort.

"Everyone's lost their mind," I said. "We're all just handling it in different ways. I let Grandma boss me around like I'm a little kid, and I have to help the Ospreys every day, but I hate being around them. Mary's a sweet kid, but I have no idea why she lives with us now. I don't know what I'm doing or what I'm going to do. I've just shut down, basically. I'm just doing it on my feet while you're doing it in bed. No difference."

"You're helping with stuff," Stephanie said with a touch of resentment in her voice. "It's not the same."

"Helping with what? Just little errands anyone could do. I have a feeling they want me to do something else, but no one will tell me what."

"What are we going to do?" Stephanie said. "We can't stay this way forever."

I chuckled a little since I wasn't that optimistic. I figured we could spend the rest of our miserable lives the same way, as an insomniac in bed and a sleepwalker in daylight. I cleared my throat to cover it, though, since I knew I needed to encourage her. Once she bathed, I'd want to be her friend.

"Well, do you want to get on your feet again?" I said.

"Yes," she said.

"Then we'll do it in small steps. Each day you can do one thing you feel you can't do. Maybe it's just sitting up in bed.

Maybe it's going for a walk. Maybe it's bathing. Once you're rehabilitated, you can decide with your own true mind."

"How will you get your true mind back?"

"No idea. Once you're feeling better, maybe you can help me figure it out." I really did hope it would work out that way. I needed help, and she was the only person in Grandma's tiny sparse neighborhood who had any chance of understanding me.

"You could stop going to the Ospreys if you don't like them."

"They have a garden, though, and Grandma says I need tasks so I don't lose my mind."

"Can't you plant your own garden?"

"I think we will, but we need all we can get before winter comes. That's what Grandma says. Anyway, the Ospreys are probably good at heart. Maybe they just miss their sons, so they take it out on us. They told me how all three live in different states, but they seem sure they're on their way here for their parents."

A twitch of life came over Stephanie. She leaned on her elbow and smiled a little. "They only have two sons now. They had three, but one killed the other."

"Why? But why?"

"I don't know. I just heard that from your Grandma, but she wouldn't tell me much more. Maybe they're in denial or something, pretending like it never happened and that all three kids are alive. You should ask your Grandma. She has too many tricks up her sleeve. It's like she's playing chess with a bunch of geese."

"And we're the geese?"

"Seems so," Stephanie said, settling down into the fetal position again.

I assured her she'd taken a good small step by letting me

into her bedroom. She promised to take more small steps on subsequent days.

It occurred to me I could be honest with her if we were going to be friends. Even if I was wrong, perhaps I could tell her the truth. "I hate to say it, Stephanie, but it smells bad in here."

She laughed a little. "Well, that's some motivation. Come back to see me in three days, and I promise it will smell at least a little bit better."

On my way out, I handed little Andrew the basket of vegetables. It was the least I could do. They didn't have the same resources we had, and they looked like they could use Vitamin C.

A thunderstorm threatened in the distance as I walked home. It was the second time I was coming home empty-handed, but this time I knew how I'd lost my payment. I tried to summon up some store of inner strength to face Grandma, to tell her I gave up food meant for our household and to insist that she be more candid with me.

In that state of mind, it felt like I was arriving home for the first time. I noticed things, the white paint peeling off the siding revealing a dull gray underneath... the beauty of the bright green door... the vines rippling like snakes traveling around the windows. She hadn't kept things up too well, and yet the place had charm.

It was a mystery to me why Grandma garnered so much respect from people, why they didn't see her as an old lady who needed help. They saw her as the one to help them. No one thought of me that way. I hadn't inherited Grandma's cloak of assurance.

I opened the door, which she only locked at night, and found Mary sitting alone at the kitchen table with a doll in her lap.

"Hey, kid! Where's Grandma?"

Mary shrugged, never taking her eyes off her doll. She was pretending to feed it some of her protein bar.

It was an old rag doll, dusty and worn, with tiny eyes of gnarled blue thread. The mouth was embroidered in red and white to make it look like she was smiling with her teeth.

"Where did you get that?" I said.

"Grandma found her in a box upstairs. I have to take care of her now."

I sat down at the table and took a protein bar from the box at the center of the table. She watched me like she didn't quite trust me, and it occurred to me that she might be easier to understand than Grandma.

"Are you happy here?" I said.

She didn't answer. It was the kind of general question a kid wouldn't want to answer, which I should have known.

I tried again. "Do you miss your parents and brothers?"

She shrugged, keeping her eyes on her doll, continually offering it crumbs.

I chewed at my flavorless protein bar, trying to think of a question she might be willing to answer. "Do you have any questions for me?" I finally asked, thinking maybe it would draw her out. Quiet children have a lot of unasked questions rolling around (I know, because I was one).

She thought for a minute, staring at my face like there was something hidden there. "What's down in the cellar?" she said.

It was an innocent question, but it gave me a jolt. I spent a lot of time banishing underground questions from my mind. "The cellar has canned goods and food in jars, all set aside so we can still eat even though the power's out and we can't go to the store."

"I know that. I mean the place below it."

"Did Grandma tell you about that?"

She shook her head.

"Then how did you know?"

She shrugged, and I felt a surge of anger. I leaned closer to her.

"Tell me the truth, Mary! How did you know about the place below the cellar? Who told you?"

She dropped the rest of the protein bar on the floor so she could use both hands to hold her doll close. Her chin quivered.

I felt guilty, of course, though I hadn't threatened her or said anything mean to her. Clearly, Mary was a very sensitive little girl, just as I'd been at her age.

Grandma sprang through the side door into the kitchen. She was wearing her lightest summer pants and a polyester blouse, like she could have been going to work at an office, but she was carrying two big duffel bags. One she placed on the floor beside the door, and the other she placed on the kitchen table. She unpacked five plastic jugs of water from it.

"All filtered from the creek. The process takes a while."

"Great," I said.

"Where are your vegetables from today's work at the Ospreys?"

The sound of a cackling bird distracted me. It was close to the house, swooping its soft wings against the glass. We turned to look, and something softened in us all. We weren't going to fight that day, not all three of us (four if you counted the doll).

"I stopped by Stephanie's," I said. "She wasn't doing well at all, so I left the vegetables with her. For Vitamin C or something. And she told me something strange about the Osprey boys. About what one did to the other."

"One of them killed the other," Mary said, which shocked me.

"Why do you tell these things to everyone but me?" I asked Grandma.

"Shush, both of you," Grandma said, waving us away. "No bloody talk. It's almost dinner time. I give out information freely. But there are some who should know more without asking. Now, Jane, do you feel guilty about all that we have here? Is that why you gave away our vegetables?"

"I guess." I looked at the doll's strange face so I wouldn't have to see Grandma's sharp eyes.

"It's something to examine about yourself," Grandma said. I wanted to know more about the Ospreys, but I didn't want her to yell at me, so I let the whole matter drop.

"Did this doll belong to Mom?" I said, gesturing at the thing.

"Yes," Grandma said. "Is that all right?"

"Shouldn't you have offered it to me first?"

"I have another doll of your mother's to give you." That was a relief, at least. I didn't really want that doll. It would have kept me up at night to have it anywhere in my room.

She disappeared from the room, and Mary surveyed me suspiciously, clutching her doll even closer so that I couldn't see its face.

Grandma returned with a different kind of doll. It was cloth as well, but it was child-sized, as big as Mary. When Mary saw it, she jumped up from the kitchen table and ran over to give it a hug, but Grandma held it high over her head.

"This one is for Jane. Her mother made it especially for her."

I went to the big doll and grabbed it, looking for something to remind me of Mom. The strangest thing about the doll was that all the fabric and threads used were various shades of blue. The skin was sky blue, the eyes and hair dark blue, the mouth navy. It wasn't cute. I figured I'd have to hide it under my bed at night so it wouldn't creep me out, but knowing Mom made it meant I had to keep it close. I choked back tears when I took the thing in my arms, in spite of its appearance.

"Why can't I have it?" Mary said.

"This one is special. It was the last thing Jane's mom did before she died."

Mary started to cry, which relieved enough pressure in the room that I didn't feel like crying anymore. It made me feel gentler towards her, so I knelt down and told her that our dolls could be friends and play together.

"I'm the kid. I should have both dolls!"

"You don't understand. You have a mother who's alive. I don't," I said.

"Is my mom still my mom?" Mary said, whimpering in a way that made me pity her after all.

"Yes, she's still your mom," Grandma said. "You can see her again before long. But right now, we have to concentrate on survival. We can't be too selfish, not even little kids. Keep in mind, Mary, Jane's mother made your doll as well. It's just as special."

Mary paused her tears and looked up with shining eyes. "What's special about her?"

"If you take care of her, she'll take care of you." Grandma winked at Mary, who seemed somewhat mollified.

"Maybe she's getting emotional because she lost all her toys when she left home," I said. "Doesn't she have any real dolls we can get from her house? You know, plastic ones?"

"She has those kinds of dolls at her old house," Grandma said, looking steadily at Mary. It was like they were communicating telepathically. "But she's in the life of our house for now. The dolls we have here are homemade rag dolls. That's what we have, and that's what we need."

Her tone had darkened, and it made me feel scolded even though I hadn't (to my knowledge) done anything wrong.

"You two go sit at the table with your new friends while I make dinner. Jane, you should name yours."

It felt so strange being ordered to play. Mary encouraged me to offer my doll some of the protein bar, but warned me not to give her any water. She didn't explain why not, but she seemed serious about it, so I played along. After several minutes of awkwardness, I began to feel less self-conscious and decided to play for Mary's sake. I learned she'd named her doll "Laura" after her favorite character in *Little House on the Prairie*. That made me feel bad for not reading to her more, so I told her I'd read her a chapter every night.

"You could name your doll after one of the other characters in the book...if you want to." Mary gave me her cute little smile, and I could see how cunning she was. Later she might use her intelligence for something more significant than playing with dolls.

I sat back and thought. "There's Mary, her sister. I always liked her. She has the same name as you, though. Would that be weird?"

Mary paused to consider it. "It's a good name. You could also name her Carrie if you want. Or Ma and Pa. Or Jack, after the dog."

"Yes. I suppose the truth is, I like Mary the best. So if it's okay with you, I'll name my doll Mary," I said.

Grandma turned around from stoking the fire to give me a proud smile. A wave of relief washed over me. I'd chosen the right name.

While Grandma was boiling water for spaghetti, we heard someone whistling in the distance. The whistling came closer to the house. Maybe it was just a neighbor, but it put me on high alert. I peeked out the living room window, and Mary joined me to see what was happening. I saw a familiar handsome face: Pastor Dan, my friend from what felt like the distant past. He was pushing his wheelbarrow full of demon jars, which I would have hated to see under any other circumstances. As it was, my heart leapt into my throat, and I ran outside to greet him.

"Dan!" I shouted out to him. "Pastor Dan!"

"Hi Jane, how do you do?" he called out, and I went out to the yard to meet him with Grandma and Mary at my heels.

"I've been better," I said.

He gave us one of his church smiles, teeth showing, friendly without being flirty. He had padded the wheelbarrow with blankets, packed in around the jars. Of all the things to rescue from the end of the world!

"What are you doing here?" The desperation I'd felt about getting married or whatever while I was in town, at my job, at church, had faded away. Dan was good-looking, but that was all there was to it.

"I bet you weren't expecting me. But then again, maybe you were! You're the smartest girl I know."

Sadly, he was probably telling the truth. "I mean, I'm glad to see you!" I said. "But why did you come here?"

"You know how dangerous these things are. I told you, demons are the mighty ribbons that will be untied at the end of the world."

I didn't remember him saying that, and I didn't even care how stupid it sounded. I needed a friend like nothing else. "But why did you bring them to me?"

He laughed. "Don't you remember? You said your Grandma was a witch."

"I never said a thing like that!" I shushed him, waving the

words away. The truth was, I had sometimes wondered if Grandma was a witch. It had occurred to me many times, but I didn't like to think about it, and I definitely wouldn't speak it out loud.

"You did! It was a prayer request you shared."

I tried to think back to a time I would have told him that. "Was it something I wrote on an anonymous card during the morning service?"

"Those aren't anonymous to us," he said, winking at me just like Grandma had.

"She's always been a scared little thing!" Grandma said behind me.

I turned around to gauge how mad she was, but she seemed all right.

"Why would you want someone you think is a witch to handle all these demons?" I asked him. "Wouldn't you want the head pastor?"

I have no idea where that man ran off to," he said. "And I can't keep these just anywhere."

Pastor Dan rested his wheelbarrow on our driveway for a moment and put his hands over his heart to address Grandma. It was a move the pastors often made when closing a sermon. "Ma'am, if I could beseech you, would you mind finding a safe place for these jars which are filled with rare demon specimens, including one very special jar that contains the demon who possessed Ted Bundy?"

I looked at Mary to see if she was scared, but she seemed more fascinated than troubled. She looked at the pile of jars eagerly, like she wanted to get her hands on them, but I guess she knew she'd be scolded if she touched them.

"Well, these are times of trouble when every man must help his neighbor," Grandma said. "So I must help you, too.

Besides, you're a friend of Jane's, so I can't turn you down. I do have a good deal of storage space in my cellar."

The idea of Dan's demon jars in our creepy cellar gave me an unpleasant shock. At first, I was afraid she meant he should take them to the cellar below, but she didn't. She led Dan down the stairs and showed him some empty shelves, and then he carried his colorful jars down an armful at a time. I held the candle, but otherwise I didn't help. I was glad to see him, to see anyone from back home, but I still didn't like the idea of toting around those crazy jars.

"Are you sure they'll be safe here?" he asked Grandma as he stacked them on the shelves. "There really are demons in here. Not everyone gets that. They think it's some kind of joke."

"Oh, I believe you," Grandma said. "They'll be safer here than anywhere. I'm no common witch like my granddaughter apparently thinks, but I know a thing or two about evil spirits and how to get rid of them. Good spirits, too. Spirits aren't meant to be contained forever, so when you're ready to let go of those jars, I can help you."

He seemed comforted by Grandma's certainty and continued stacking.

When we went back upstairs, I set an extra place at the table for him.

WHILE WE ATE Grandma's spaghetti, I plied him for information. "How are my roommates? Bea? Penny?" I'd been lonely for their company, and I kept hoping I'd go back to them or that they could come to live at Grandma's house.

"They were fine last I spoke to them, but they're gone now," he said. "Everyone who could has gotten out of the city.

We're running out of food there fast, and let's just say it doesn't smell too nice. Your old apartment is empty."

I'd probably never return to that life now, and it would only live in my memories. I found myself shedding a few tears. No one knew what to say to me, so as I wiped my tears away with my cloth napkin, they ate their food twice as fast.

Grandma found a way to bring the subject back to what interested her about Dan. "When did you start seeing demons? Jane tells me you only joined her church a few years ago. Was it after becoming a member that you started seeing demons?"

"Even before that," he said. "I guess you could say those jars brought me to the Lord in the first place. I had started seeing the little creatures lots of places. Some looked like little ghost rats and bugs, but some were like twigs and stones. I met with all kinds of religious people, from priests to psychics, trying to get an idea of what to do about the things. I could tell they were evil. I could feel it in my very soul. Before that, I hadn't even known I had a soul."

Mary regarded Dan and his demon stories with wide eyes, clutching her doll close. "Isn't it Mary's bedtime?" I said. "These kinds of stories might upset kids."

"Most kids, maybe, but not Mary," Grandma said, waving me off. She gestured for Dan to continue his explanation.

"So," he said, "I decided that if those evil things were all over the place, they ought to be put away. I tried various methods, spells and prayers, but nothing seemed to work. I started capturing them in jars, but the demons would disappear out of the jars once I turned my head. I had to experiment until I hit upon a couple of solutions. For one thing, I joined the Idlewild Community Church. I'd grown up Methodist, but you know how it is. I liked the folks I met there, and something about being in the church building gave me a renewed spirit. It spread throughout my life. Then I started putting construction paper in the glass jars, so the demons couldn't see out. I think it was the combination of the church and the construction paper that helped me finally trap them."

"Why do you think it's your duty to capture these things?" Grandma said. "Why not leave it to someone with more seniority, more wisdom?"

Her line of questioning might have seemed rude to a stranger, but I could tell she was taking him seriously, which surprised me.

Dan thought for a second, looking around the house for the right words. "It's just, I know no one else can take care of it. I can see the little creatures, and most people can't. Why God gave it to me to see them and not to others, I don't know. He didn't give me the words to persuade folks, either."

Finally, Grandma cracked a smile at him, and I knew he'd passed some sort of test in her eyes. I rarely passed her tests myself.

"You're right to take care of them yourself," she said. "When a job isn't being done, it's time to pick up your own set of tools and do what you can. Otherwise, who is going to help all the poor souls out there?"

Dan leaned back and basked in her understanding. As far as I knew, it was rare for someone to understand someone else. A special thing the two shared. Although I doubted if he could ever understand her in return.

I asked him for more information about the Disaster and my old friends and acquaintances from church, but he didn't have much more—only that everyone had been devastated and scared once we lost power for so long. They'd all been anxious to get somewhere else. People who lived on the streets all had shelter after taking over abandoned apartments."

"You'll stay here, won't you?" I said. "We need all the help we can get."

He hesitated. "It'll take me several trips just to move these jars. But I enjoyed the journey out here, so I might just go back and forth for a while. I feel freer than I've ever felt, really."

Excuses. He was determined to abandon me.

"I wish I felt that way. I miss my old life," I confessed. I didn't mean to hurt Grandma, but I missed my friends and my apartment.

Pastor Dan gave a sort of sympathetic grunt, but I could see he didn't feel what I felt.

"Jane loves an easy path, but she'll get used to this," Grandma said. "It's a good life, once you learn how to live it."

Mary and Pastor Dan seemed to know what she was talking about, but I had no idea. Didn't I know how to live my own life?

6

DAN AND HIS WHEELBARROW WERE GONE BY THE TIME I woke up the next morning. He was much more industrious than I was when it came to gathering those jars.

Just as I was about to walk out the door on my way to the Ospreys, Grandma approached me with the blue doll held out before her. She pushed it at me and insisted I take it with me, but I crossed my arms. Humiliation upon humiliation!

"I don't know what you're up to," I said, "but I'm not going to embarrass myself in front of them again."

She stepped closer to me, and I got a whiff of some familiar scent, something boggy and citrusy at the same time. She must have been at the creek before I was even awake. She was hard-working, but that didn't mean I had to do everything she said.

"Jane, I can't explain a talisman to you like it's a stick of deodorant you'd buy at the store. If I did, it might not work. Too much awareness drains their power. Trust me, though, work is no fun without a friend to pass the time. You will want that doll."

"I'm too old to believe a doll is my friend, or a magic talisman. You've been acting so weird lately, Grandma."

She shook her head. "You have no faith, child. That's your problem."

"I'm the one who goes to church, not you," I said. "I mean, *went*."

While we fought quietly by the front door, Mary had wandered into the living room carrying her own doll.

"Jane," she said in a sweet, imploring voice, "if you're not going to take Mary with you, can I have her today? She and Laura could play together."

I couldn't blame the girl for loving those ugly dolls. What else did she have to do? "You can have her until I get home," I said.

Grandma told me I was a fool, but she gave Doll Mary to the girl Mary. "Jane will want to take the doll with her tomorrow," she told her. "Just wait and see what a pickle she gets into. Some people have to learn the hard way."

I had enough strange faith in Grandma to feel unsettled on my way to the Ospreys. They seemed normal enough when I arrived, but what proved unusual was the amount of work for the day. They led me to the backyard and tasked me with my normal watering and weeding as well as giving the bathrooms and kitchen a deep clean and then baking a cake.

"It's our son's birthday tomorrow," Mr. Osprey said. "We want everything to be perfect, just in case he makes it home."

"Which son?" I said, wondering about the rumor I'd heard from Stephanie.

"His name is Vern," Mrs. Osprey said, giving me a sad smile. "I know what you must be thinking, but he wouldn't be interested in someone like you."

It was better not to talk to her. I went about my work as quickly as I could, rushing through my gardening and bathroom-cleaning, but my energy flagged as I began cleaning the kitchen. The afternoon wore on, and still I toiled. I began to feel so tired I was afraid I'd melt away.

While I mopped the kitchen tile, Mr. Osprey interrupted to ask me to rescrub the shower grout in both bathrooms. "I won't tell Mrs. Osprey, but I'd skedaddle and do it before she finds out."

He leaned on the bench near the knife block, and I wanted to take the biggest one and plunge it into his soft, open hands. I didn't like the way I was starting to feel about the Ospreys. It wasn't just the chores. It was their sense of entitlement, of specialness, when we all needed to band together to try to survive. But I almost felt guilty when I considered that they'd lost a child. Maybe that had made them feel they were owed something in return.

When Mr. Osprey followed me into the bathroom, supposedly to show me what he wanted me to redo, he closed the door behind us and pulled me into a hug. I pushed him away, and he gave me a look of hurt surprise.

"I thought we were getting along so well," he said.

"No touching me," I said.

"You're so alone out here. There are only two grown men among us, don't you realize? Enough of us to go around, though." He pulled me into another hug, but I twisted away and opened the door, calling for Mrs. Osprey. When she came into the bathroom, I thought about telling her about his unwanted advances, but I knew he'd just deny it anyway—and after that, I just wanted to finish my work and go home. So I pivoted and asked her for advice on cleaning the grout the way she wanted.

"Everyone knows you have to use an old toothbrush," she said, and she found one for me.

They left me alone, mercifully, while I took a toothbrush to both bathrooms.

I hated being somewhere where it seemed like everyone hated me and only wanted to use me in some way. Maybe that's why Grandma had told me to bring the doll along, to serve as a source of love in a hostile place. I wished I could find a less obvious talisman, something I could slip into my pocket. My mom hadn't left me anything else, though.

Dinnertime was closing in by the time I finished cleaning the kitchen. Mrs. Osprey began to cook in her fire pit outside while I started on the cake on a table she'd set up nearby. I wondered if I was expected to join them for dinner. She made her tomatoes into a sauce with chopped onions, ignoring me while I made the cake mix. It was a soft yellow cake with a plastic tub of chocolate icing waiting to be spread on top.

"What will we use as an egg substitute?" I asked. "I read somewhere you can whip up the juice from a can of chickpeas as a substitute."

She looked over at me with a frown. "Check the cupboard, bottom left. There are eggs in there."

There was a basket of them, all slightly different shades of brown.

"I didn't see any chickens out there," I said.

"No, indeed. Our friend has them."

"A friend? From where?"

"We have friends other than you, Miss Nosy," she said, returning to her sauce.

I bit my tongue and returned to my work, pouring the batter into a sheet cake pan and covering it with foil. I put it on the rack above the fireplace next to Mrs. Osprey's sauce and sat in one of the lawn chairs surrounding the fireplace while it baked. Mrs. Osprey sat in front of me, closer to the fire, guarding her sauce.

The sun was sinking low in the sky, and the auroras had turned from greenish to blueish, which Grandma said was a bad sign. Something about heightened solar activity. I still had no idea what the sun was doing to spawn the strange colors, but I was growing increasingly distrustful of the sun.

"Do you want me to frost it too?" I said.

Mrs. Osprey turned her head around very slowly. "Of course! What do you mean?"

"I mean, it's getting late. I'm usually only here during the day." I'd never walked back to Grandma's house alone in the dark. I supposed it was safe enough, but the idea frightened me.

"Do you have a hot date tonight?" she sneered and turned her attention back to her sauce.

While I was hating her, her husband came out of the house with a can of beans in one hand and two eggs in the other.

"I think your cake is ready. I can smell it," Mrs. Osprey said.

I took the cake pan from the fire and set it on the grass, praying it would cool quickly so I could get out of there. I swore to myself that I'd tell Grandma I wouldn't come back. I'd figure out a way to plant my own garden somehow. Or else, get scurvy. Vegetables weren't worth a day with the Ospreys. Besides, I'd yet to successfully bring any home.

"Mr. Osprey, would you mind frosting this cake for me?" I said. "I think I should be getting on home. Grandma will be worried about me."

"Hon, you'll have to ask Mrs. Osprey," he said.

I rolled my eyes. They were acting like they were my parents. Mom always used to tell me to ask Grandma, like she was the final word. "I already asked her," I said, and shivered. But I wasn't cold. No, I was furious. I wanted them both to die. If I could have poisoned them then, I swear, I would have.

And for what? Simply for being rude to me. I wasn't wearing handcuffs. I could walk off whenever I wanted, right? I could walk back to my apartment in the city and find a way to live out the last of days with whoever remained there. If these really were the last of days.

I felt a pull, though, a weight in my ankles. Instead of asking Mrs. Osprey, I watched the sky grow darker and waited for the cake to cool. With no light pollution to interfere, the colors were too bright and there were too many stars. It was unnerving, like the night had a cosmic pox. I preferred the sky to be quotidian and comfortable, a warm blue or cool violet in the background of my life that I didn't have to think about. Without electric lights, the sky was becoming far too prominent in my life.

"Daydreaming?" Mr. Osprey called out to me, laughing.

"She's a dreamer, all right," Mrs. Osprey said, and it didn't sound like a complete insult.

Since they seemed softer than before, I decided to do something bold for a change. "Do you two dislike me for some reason?" I asked them.

They looked at each other in shock.

"Why on earth would you say that?" Mr. Osprey said.

"She's paranoid," muttered Mrs. Osprey.

"What is it you really want from me? You know your sons aren't really going to arrive from so far away, don't you? Why make me do so much work?"

Their mouths opened like fish. Then Mrs. Osprey began to cry. Instead of answering me, she ran inside.

"Aw, why'd you have to go say that?" Mr. Osprey said. "She just needed something to look forward to."

"But we all do!" I said. "Why are your feelings more important than ours?"

He didn't answer me. He stared into the fire. Perhaps someone could have asked me that question as well. Who knew how much suffering had occurred throughout the county, state, country, world? I had no idea. And yet, I was worried about the Ospreys hurting my feelings. I wished I could amputate my feelings so I could get around better.

When the cake cooled, I frosted it and left without saying goodbye.

I walked the dirt road with no light but the partial moon and the auroras, poised above like sentient sky snakes. Once or twice, I was sure I heard another pair of footsteps behind me, but when I turned around to look, no one was there. The trees hung over me, reminding me of shadow people who stood over my bed as a child. Sometimes the shadow people were Mom and Grandma, but sometimes they were strangers.

"That's silly," I said out loud. "It's stupid, actually."

I continued on until I reached Stephanie's trailer. I'd avoided their place that morning since she asked me to give her three days to get herself together. This time, though, I was the one who needed the favor. There was no sign they were awake—no fire or candlelight—but I crept up to the trailer door and knocked.

The oldest one, Charles, answered. He held a lit candle in a little blue tin. It gave off a sickly-sweet vanilla scent.

"Hello," I said. "I was just passing by."

He stared at me, waiting. How could I explain myself?

His little brother crept into the tiny living room behind him. "Hello," Andrew whispered. "Could you come inside so we can close the door? There's a lot of mosquitos."

I did as requested. I had nothing to offer, no basket of vegetables.

"Mom's asleep, but I can wake her up," Andrew said.

"That's okay. To tell you the truth, I only stopped here because I got scared. I worked late at the Ospreys, so I was walking home in the dark, without a light."

The boys looked down. What I was admitting was shameful to them.

"I should be on my way," I said. "Thanks, though."

Before I could open the door to leave, Stephanie crept out into the hall, holding what looked like a small child. A shadow child. As she approached me, though, I saw it was something more familiar: the blue doll I'd named Mary. Her navy-blue thread mouth stood out even in the darkness, like a shoreline at night.

"How did you get that?" I said, already knowing the answer.

"Your Grandma left it here for you. She said you'd need it and thought you'd take a break from the Ospreys and come by sooner. I guess you never take a break while you're there, though! You're nicer to them than I could be."

Nice! I'd been intimidated by the Ospreys, not nice. I reached out for the doll, and Stephanie put her into my arms. The fabric was warm, like Stephanie had been clutching it for a long time. I wondered if it was wrong to take the doll away from her, since she needed a talisman, too. When I brought the doll to my face, though, I smelled flowers. I didn't know the distinct smells of different flowers. All I can say is that the doll, Mary, smelled like flowers, and Stephanie, who still hadn't bathed, did not.

"I don't understand Grandma," I said to Stephanie and the two boys.

"She's a strange lady," Stephanie said. "But she's taking care of everyone in the best way she can. She always tells me that she can't command the sun and the rain. Or the nation-states, or electricity. Just like she can't make her leg grow back. There's a lot she can do somehow, though. It's like she knows a little magic."

The boys slunk back, like they were uncomfortable talking about Grandma. Perhaps they were uncomfortable around me, a woman who barged into their dark house at night to collect a hideous doll.

The doll was starting to look pretty to me, though. Mom had made her strangely, but the best she could. I told people my mother had a serious mental illness, and that was true, but it wasn't all that was true about her. She was funny and kind. She played with me. There was a kind of light she had, and once she died, I never found it anywhere else. Not in Grandma, not in myself. Some beauties are born in only one person, and they die with that person.

"I'm sorry. I'll go home now," I said.

"Come back and see me! Just a little more time, and I promise I'll be better. I'm proud of myself for getting out of bed to give this to you."

"Me too. You've been nice to me."

On the dark road back to Grandma's house, I hugged my doll and felt braver than before. There was something strange about the doll. It was more than its odd appearance. It did seem to have a kind of power I could feel, something that coursed through my veins. I could feel the doll's love somehow as I walked home.

"I hate myself, though," I said to the doll. I'd fought hard to grow up, and now I was surrendering to someone else's backwards fantasy, the doldrums of youth. Or so it seemed to me as I trotted back to Grandma.

When I got home, Mary was already asleep, but Grandma was waiting up for me. She scooped me a bowl of bean chili still hot from the fire.

"Grandma," I said as I waited for the food to cool. "Why are you making me do all this?"

"I didn't make the sun act up. If that hadn't happened, you'd still be living in your apartment and working at the library right now, and I'd still be enjoying my hobbies in comfort. We've both lost a lot."

"I'm tired of losing," I said, tearing up a little.

"You'll feel better after you eat."

That kind of advice always annoyed me, since it only papered over the hole in the wall, but I did what she said, and I did feel better.

"We are in a bad situation that could get worse," she said. "You haven't thought of all the bad things that can happen yet, but I have. I haven't told you all I'm thinking because I don't want to scare you."

"I'm scared anyway. I can't help it. I want you to tell me what you know." I gestured to Doll Mary, who I'd sat up in the chair beside me. "I don't want to be a child forever." The words felt like a promise as I said them.

"This doll won't make you a child! Your mother was a troubled woman, but she was also wise. I couldn't share my responsibilities with her, but she had her own talents. You should take whatever gifts you can from her."

"Share some of your responsibilities with me. Maybe we can get out of this mess."

"We can't turn the power back on. But there are other messes you don't know about. What do you say we take it a little at a time?"

"Fine," I said.

Grandma sliced an apple for me, like she hadn't heard what I said about feeling like a child. Still, I ate the slices.

"I'll tell you what our first step is," she said.

"I bet I can guess," I said. "You want me to take my doll to the Ospreys tomorrow."

She clapped her hands and laughed, and for a minute she reminded me of holiday Grandma, the one who'd wrapped presents and played Santa Claus when I was little.

"That's right," she said. "The doll is more than she seems."

With that in mind, I went to bed with the doll beside me, not hidden anymore, her strange head resting on the pillow next to mine.

That night, another bad solar storm blazed through the sky. Mary cried out, and Grandma got up to comfort her, but I stayed still in bed and held onto my doll.

7

Grandma told me to keep the doll hidden from the Ospreys at first, since it would be funnier that way. She gave me one of my old backpacks from high school and stuffed the doll into it along with a bottle of water and a protein bar. The way she'd planned it all out, it felt like a practical joke.

"When they tell you to work, wait until you're alone, and then give the doll food and water. That will give the doll strength to work for you," she said.

She had lost her mind, but I was too tired to resist. "Fine, even though you sound like a crazy person."

"Can I ask you a question?" she said before I opened our front door.

"I wish you would."

"You went to church before. You talk about faith. But where's your faith now? Did you lose it in the incident?"

I thought for a minute. "I've prayed for God to help us so many times, but it feels like God is busy right now. For some reason."

Grandma nodded. “That’s why we need something tangible.”

I was too tired to debate theological matters with her on top of everything else. As I made my way to the Ospreys, I wondered where she got her energy from at her age. Maybe missing one leg made her lighter. It was sad that she wouldn’t be getting any more new-and-improved prosthetic legs, and nor would anyone else. That is, unless someone got the world’s machinery going again.

The path that had been so ominous the night before had become bright and airy again. We were in the stretch of late summer where early morning was the only cool part of the day. I didn’t know what day it was, to tell the truth, and I didn’t want to know. Maybe it didn’t matter anymore. Only the seasons mattered, when to sow and when to reap.

The Ospreys didn’t answer my knock on their door, but it was unlocked so I let myself in. I found them outside, drinking from mugs and staring into their fire pit. Without the doll, I would have been afraid of them. Why had I been afraid of them, of their judgment and disdain? I couldn’t say. All I knew was that the doll was stronger than I was, and it gave me small pulses of strength through the canvas of my backpack.

I stood near them and the fire for a minute before Mrs. Osprey broke the silence.

“You’ll be glad to know my son couldn’t make it last night. He was too busy with work this time, but he’ll be here for us soon.”

“You have a CB radio?” I said.

Mrs. Osprey smiled, and her husband looked away. “I have something better,” she said. “I can read minds. When people let me, anyway.”

“I see.” I hadn’t realized she was so disconnected from

reality. I would have hated her less and had more compassion if I'd known.

"I know it sounds kooky," Mr. Osprey said, throwing up his hands. "But it's true."

"My son found a car, and he's leaving soon to come get us," she said. "He has to take care of some business first, but he's going to get here. Just wait and see."

"Won't it be hard to get here from such a long way away? With the roads blocked?"

"Yes," she hissed. "But still, he'll find a way. Wait and see, Miss Know-it-all." She stood up and gestured for me to follow her to the house. "It's about time you get to work, isn't it?"

That day, in addition to the gardening, she wanted me to cook ten loaves of bread to share with the three other households, and to take her water filtration system and a trash bag filled with empty plastic jugs down to the creek to replenish their supply. I knew my doll heard the orders, and I kept my backpack on as I carried the water stuff down the path to the creek behind the Ospreys' house.

Once I was alone, I unzipped my backpack and brought out Doll Mary. She slumped in the grass, her head falling into a patch of purple weeds. I felt like crying, and I was so frustrated that I forgot what I was supposed to do. For that minute, or maybe it was ten or twenty, maybe it was more, I stared at her soft blue skin and hated myself for being such a fool.

But Grandma told me to give her food and drink, so I unwrapped the protein bar, put it to her mouth, and then offered her a sip from the water bottle. I have no idea if she really drank or ate. Do statues drink offered milk? Do gods taste roasted meat?

Something happened, though. Peace for a while, the creek in all my senses, bog and lemon lukewarm cocktail, fishwings scum slime darkness, gripsalt shadowbright dappled and foam, and cool shadow, and deep balloon alabaster dolomite gypsum sand, and beneath all sediment the stone that expands.

It wasn't long at all like that. Doll Mary was moving for me while I was somewhere underwater, and when I came up for breath, my shorts and T-shirt were lying on the bank of the creek, and Doll Mary was lying there like a sack.

I pulled myself out of the cool water and got dressed, getting my clothes wet without a second thought. The bottles of water were full, the water filtration gear clean. Grandma was right about the doll working for me. When I went back to the Ospreys house, would I find the gardenwork finished and the loaves of bread baked too? The sun was past the noonpoint, but not too low in the sky. What a perfect day, the sun warming my wet clothes.

Indeed, my work was finished. The garden beds were lush yet clear of weeds, three full baskets of vegetables had been harvested, and the kitchen smelled like rosemary and yeast. The Ospreys treated me like nothing was wrong, like a two-foot blue doll had not been the one responsible for all their needful labor. She must have worn my skin like a suit, or something like that. She'd definitely used my clothes. Good for her!

And while my work was done, I'd been in a beautiful holding place.

My mother's trick. Her blessing.

I stuffed Doll Mary back in my backpack along with some vegetables and loaves of bread and said my goodbyes.

I didn't even hate the Ospreys on my way home. My wet clothes and the shade trees kept me cool along the path, and I thought about stopping at Stephanie's house, but she'd wanted more time to make progress. Yes, I would give her that!

The road curved, and I had a new appreciation for Grandma's house as it came into sight. The chipped exterior, the little door. Smoke from the chimney. Someone home. Hydrangeas and coneflowers blooming in all shades of pink, buzz and song of the outside everywhere, all these things I usually struggle to notice.

But when I opened the door, I was surprised by a sad sight. Mary was in Grandma's lap curled into a ball, crying desperately. After so much luck, how could sadness enter our house?

"What happened?" I said.

"Mary's family," Grandma said. "They've moved on."

"Moved where?" It was strange I hadn't heard any news about them, hadn't asked about them. I'd just accepted Mary was part of our house.

"They left a note behind," Grandma said. "It's on the kitchen table if you want to see."

I didn't, but I read it anyway. It said:

To Mary's New Family:

We decided to move. Jeremiah's cousin has acreage. We're so sorry we didn't come say goodbye. It was too hard. We know Mary has to stay behind, and we couldn't say goodbye again. We know you will take good care of her. Someday when she's ready, if we all survive this madness, please let her visit us.

Love,

Mary's Old Family

"Dang," I said. "That's sad." The "Mary's Old Family" seemed a touch passive-aggressive. Did they think we'd taken her away from them on purpose? And too sad to say goodbye? It made no sense to me. It sounded like they were escaping something and didn't want us to know. The handwriting reminded me a bit of Grandma's, messy like hers but sloped the other way. Maybe people who lived out in the woods by choice didn't take much pride in neat handwriting.

"They don't deserve Mary," Grandma whispered, as though the child couldn't hear.

"Why don't they want me?" Mary said, still crying into Grandma's arm without looking up.

"It's my fault, Mary," Grandma said, tears springing to her eyes as well. "If I hadn't taken you in when you were ill, you'd still be with them. But you'll be glad someday. Sooner rather than later, I imagine."

All the tears made me feel like I was stuck in a humid room before a thunderstorm. "Can I help with anything?"

"You could get dinner on the table," Grandma said. "Go down to the cellar and get whatever you want. And just remember, while you're at it, you could always go farther below. Whenever you're ready."

The beautiful experience I'd had with Doll Mary, who was still in the backpack I wore, felt far away, but it kept me calm. I lit a candle and descended.

As I passed through the dark space, I searched the floor for a passageway to that cellar below the cellar. I didn't see one, but I had the feeling I wasn't looking hard enough. Something stopped me, though, and reminded me of my duty. It must have been Doll Mary giving me a little kick through the fabric of the backpack. I picked out a couple of boxes of macaroni and cheese from the shelves.

Back upstairs, I filled our cast-iron pot with clean water to boil and went through the motions of making the boxed meals while Grandma and Mary cried together. I had only seen Grandma cry once that I could remember, when she told me Mom was dead. Even though, unlike me, she'd been expecting her death, she'd still mourned like an ordinary person.

While the pasta cooked, I unzipped Doll Mary so she could sit on the couch with them and lend her moral support.

"Where's Laura?" I asked, surprised that Mary's ever-present doll companion wasn't there as a comfort item.

"I'm mad at her!" Mary said.

"Why?"

"She didn't tell me it was going to happen! She's told me everything else! Why didn't she tell me?" The girl collapsed into more heartrending sobs.

I stared at the back of her head, a jealous heartburn rising in my chest. Her doll must be more special than mine, because Doll Mary hadn't said a word to me. Why had Grandma given me the silent blue one? The dolls were from my mother, after all.

"The dolls are both very special," Grandma said, wiping her eyes and looking up at me. It was like she'd read my mind. "They have different personalities to suit your different needs."

The fear we were all sharing some delusion crowded out my jealousy. To distract myself, I took the bread and vegetables from my backpack and made a salad to go with the macaroni. Soon, I was setting the table, serving drinks, and even picking Mary up from Grandma's lap to put her at the table.

"I'm sorry about what happened," I told her. "But you have to eat."

I must have said it with more conviction than before, because she obeyed me for the first time. It was like I'd grown taller overnight.

While she and Grandma ate, I found Doll Laura in Mary's room and brought it out to sit in her lap. Mary gave the doll some of her macaroni, and as far as I could tell, the doll's lips didn't move to accept the food, but what did I know? I could have offered Doll Mary something, too, but I was in the mood to do the after-dinner chores myself, so I let her rest for the evening.

Late that night, I woke up to the sound of thunder (or maybe another solar storm, there was no news report to let us know), and I couldn't get back to sleep. I looked at Doll Mary lying on the pillow beside me and offered her some candy from my nightstand drawer, and then a sip from my water glass.

"Mary, can you speak to me?" I said. "Can you tell me what's going to happen?"

This time, I didn't get sleepy and slip into another world. With my own eyes, I saw the ragdoll flop around, off my bed and across the room, before slipping out my door. I didn't enjoy seeing the doll move. It was unnatural, like watching a puppet show. I wished she'd put me into a trance like she had before. I wondered if I should chase her like an escaping pet, but she soon returned with Doll Laura under her arm. She set the smaller doll on the floor and gave her a bit of food and water.

"Why do you disturb my sleep?" Doll Laura's unsightly embroidered red lips and white teeth didn't move when she spoke. It was as if her voice was being projected inside my head somehow or there was some unseen ventriloquist. Or was it magic that allowed her to speak without the machinery of speech?

"I'm worried. Everything's really bad right now," I told her. "We don't know what's going on, why the sun turned against us, and we're all miserable. And I think Grandma wants something from me, for me to go deep underground, but I don't want to. I have no idea how to make things better. My mother must have made you with magic. She's kind of like your god," I said, realizing it as I said it out loud. "Don't you owe me, her daughter, some consideration?"

"You are the daughter," she said. "But I am responsible for Mary, the little girl. That's who I was charged with. Your mother made you this doll to protect you." She gestured towards my hulking blue friend.

"She didn't make both of you for me?"

"She made me for your Grandma, this one for you." Again, Doll Laura gestured to her silent companion. "Your Grandma gave me to the little girl."

"Why?"

"For private reasons. Just as your doll would not reveal your secrets, I can't reveal the secrets of my companion."

"What are you?" I had a feeling the doll could turn around and leave me any minute, ending my audience with her, and I needed some scrap of understanding. "Why did Mom make you?

"She was dying, and she knew you would need help. She knew hard times were coming, though she didn't know exactly what or when."

"Was she a witch?" I said the word with some trepidation. I didn't like the idea.

"I won't answer that," she said. "It's a stupid question. Your mother was what she was. Anything imposed on her from the outside is someone else's idea of her."

I sat cross-legged on the floor and reached for Doll Laura like I was going to play with her, give her an empty teacup and braid her hair. She stepped out of my grasp.

"I need to return," she said.

"But Doll Laura, I mean. Laura..., what is in the cellar

below the cellar?" I regretted asking right away, because I was terrified of the answer. Part of me must have wanted to know, though.

She was silent for a moment, her gnarled yarn features glimmering in the hint of moonlight.

"Why do you want to know?"

"Grandma wants me to go down there, but I don't know what it is."

Blue Doll Mary continued to stand with us, presumably watching and listening. I had the thought then: what if I was just playing with dolls like a little kid would?

"I can take you down there now if you really want to know," Doll Laura said. "But you aren't ready yet."

"Ready how?"

"Some things are very frightening until you live enough life. Then they seem much less threatening. If you go down there now, it could kill you. I would know."

I felt a lonesome chill. Had the cellar below the cellar killed my mother somehow? I was in the presence of some bit of my mother. I wanted to hug the dolls then, but I refrained. Although they might contain fragments of Mom, they were other things as well, rag and thread, light and darkness. Doll Laura took a step back from me, as if she were about to go.

"Wait, can you answer anything else? Like, what happened the night the power went out? When will things get back to normal?"

"I have to go back now," Doll Laura said. Without a good-bye, she shuffled out of the room on her unsteady legs.

I thanked Mary for her help and put her back to bed. I had no idea if she ever slept or if she was always wide awake, waiting to be of service.

If my mother was a witch, she must have only known

child's magic, bringing playthings to life. What if her curiosity about the cellar under the cellar was too big, too old, and it killed her? I was curious about the cellar too, but I didn't want to die. A kind of mortal terror filled me as I negotiated between my desire to know and my desire to live.

⸙ 8 ⸙

As THE WEEKS PASSED, AND AS THE AURORAS FADED LIKE scars, I stopped thinking any of it was strange. Once everything is strange, nothing is. I decided not to worry for a while but to mind my own business, enjoy the summer. I grew comfortable with the animating magic imbued in my doll companion. Doll Mary did my chores while I existed in some pleasant fleshless netherworld. In the evenings after dinner, I read to Mary from whatever books I could find at Grandma's, from *Lost Horizon* to the New Testament to cheap Westerns.

Stephanie continued to improve and was soon gathering water and planting a little garden with the help of her kids. I thought the worst part of our new world was having to use bedpans at night and clean them in the morning. Stephanie thought the worst part was not having any videos to watch. The more we talked about it, the more complaints we found. Something I hadn't said to anyone was how scared I was for one of us to get really hurt or sick. How would we access medical treatment?

Once a week, Charles went to the Ospreys house in my

place to give me the day off. Their need for chores was ravenous. On my frequent visits to see Stephanie, we wondered why Grandma allowed them to have so much power over us. Just for the few vegetables they shared? There must have been more to it, but Grandma wouldn't tell us. She said we had to wait and see.

The summer began to die, yielding to autumn, and the evenings became so breezy, we left the windows open. Grandma cooked indoors rather than build a fire pit outside like the Ospreys and Stephanie's family did, but it never seemed to make our house too warm.

When winter came, life would be harder. Winters were harsh, and we'd need all the firewood we could get. We wouldn't have fresh food from the garden to supplant our diet, and the cold and snow would make traveling to each other's houses more difficult.

But when I mentioned how difficult it would be to Grandma, she dismissed my concerns. She said she had no fear of winter, because that was the time she was strongest. So I enjoyed the present, the simplicity of summer, and fell into a routine. I would venture to say I was happy, if only a little.

One morning when I arrived at the Ospreys, a battered white truck was parked outside, and the house was full of alien jubilation. One of their sons, Derek, had driven all the way from Maine just like his mother had hoped. I wondered if he was the one who had killed his brother, or the one who hadn't killed his brother. Then again, maybe it was a baseless rumor.

The Ospreys treated me like their maid, barely introducing me to their son. He was handsome, I had to admit, with serious eyes and dark wavy hair.

I got Doll Mary to do my chores, so I didn't see him that day. Whether he talked to her, I can't say, but I assumed Doll

Mary didn't do much talking even when she wore my disguise. She was the quiet type.

That evening, he offered to drive me home. Mrs. Osprey yelled at him about wasting gas (which, to be fair, had clearly become quite precious), so he walked me home instead. She objected to that as well, but nothing would stop him. I was wary of him since, according to Stephanie, either he or his living brother was a murderer, but it was nice to talk to someone new for a change.

"How long did it take you to drive here?" I asked him once we were alone.

"Ages," he said. "Lots of roads are blocked, and so many great new cars were just pushed into ditches. Took me forever to navigate without my phone, too."

"Where did you get all the gas for your truck?"

"I had a siphon to remove it from the vehicles that won't work anymore. Plus, some people are trading things. I had a truckful of useful stuff and did some odd jobs for people along the way. I sold some extra gasoline I found."

"Sounds resourceful," I said. That sort of thing wouldn't have impressed me before, but I'd come to admire it.

He was quiet for a minute. I felt Doll Mary rustling around a little in my backpack, which was worrisome. Was she warning me of something?

"I guess you've heard about my past," he said at last in a tone of weary defeat.

"I heard that someone in your family killed his brother. Was it you?"

"It was," he said.

To my shame, whatever nervousness I felt in the presence of a fratricidal killer was matched by my excitement and curiosity. Were his parents somehow to blame for his crime? I hoped so.

"How old were you? Why did you do it?"

"I was thirteen, and my brother Vern was only eleven." His voice got thick, and he stared at his hands like he still couldn't believe he'd done it. "I heard a voice I thought was from God telling me to kill my brother. It reminded me of a story from Sunday School about how God told Abraham to sacrifice his son Isaac. Abraham obeyed, because he thought God would bring Isaac back from the dead. That's what I thought would happen to Vern, that God would make things okay somehow as long as I did what he said."

"Why did you think God would want you to kill your brother?"

"I thought God was testing me." Derek looked ahead, avoiding my eyes. "When God calls you, you have to answer."

"How did you do it?" I almost whispered, starting to feel guilty for my curiosity. Derek killing his brother because of a Bible story didn't make sense to me, but he must have been insane at the time. I hoped he was only insane.

"With an ax," he muttered, like he was confessing to cheating on a test. Like he was ashamed, on one hand, but also a tiny bit proud of having the gall.

"Did you chop his head off?" I whispered even lower than before.

"I split his head in two. I didn't mean to, but he was trying to get away. I held him in my arms while he died, and I was praying God would save him the whole time." He stopped and breathed hard, like he was going to have a panic attack. "Better not talk about it anymore right now," he said.

I nodded, decided to drop the matter. There was something else I couldn't let go, even though it was comparatively petty. "Your parents have been very rude to me."

"They've been through a lot. Because of me, but also because of how jealous they are of everyone else."

He was still breathing hard, but I couldn't stop complaining about them.

"But we all have! I mean, look what's happened to us! And they act like they're the king and queen. Like their feelings matter more than anyone else's."

"They mean well," he said.

I didn't think so, and I gave him many reasons why as we walked the path back to Grandma's.

"They aren't naturally happy like you are. I just loved watching you work with that sweet little smile on your face. It was like every chore was a joy for you." He gave me an affectionate look, and I tried not to laugh. Doll Mary was the one who loved chores, not me.

Once we reached Grandma' house, I invited him inside, but he said he had to get back to his parents' house. He looked at her house like it was a loathsome place and he couldn't wait to get away.

Grandma was in a chipper mood when I went inside.

"We have a visitor in the cellar. An old friend of yours." She winked at me, and the creases in the corners of her eyes seemed smoother than usual.

I had only one old friend who had been to Grandma's cellar. I took a candle and went downstairs to find Dan adding more demon jars to our spare shelves.

"Hey there, Jane!" His friendliness made the cellar seems brighter. Or it might have been the combined strength of our two candles.

"I'm glad you made it back safely," I said. "And your jars, I guess."

He slid some of Grandma's canned soups aside to make room for the last of his jars.

"Have you been able to find enough food on your way here? Maybe when he left, we could send him off with some provisions.

"I still have some ramen and canned food left. Plus, whenever I pass a store or a gas station, I can find a few things people left behind in all the rush. Spam. Crackers. Whatever's left."

"Are the stores still open? How do you pay?"

"No, most have been emptied out or ransacked, but I know a few where you can still trade for food. I trade them paper towels or something."

"Sounds like things are bad out there."

"You don't want to find out."

I heard the strange sound below me. Maybe it was more like bellowing than gears.

"Did you hear that?" I said.

He cocked his head. "Yeah, I heard something. I've asked Grandma about it before, but she says that's her domain—and yours."

I wanted to tell him that she wasn't his grandma to call Grandma, but I let it go. Maybe we had to share everything in this new world. "What did she tell you? What did she say was down there?

"She told me that once you go downstairs, you might be the one to help me get rid of these jars, but only if you get brave enough to see what's down there first."

"It must be awful down there, Dan. I can almost smell the fumes from here. That place gives me some kind of vibrations in my bones, and it almost hurts me. And yet all she'll tell me is that I need go there to see it for myself."

Dan gave me his kind look, the one he'd used as youth pastor. "Parents and grandparents are hard to understand, Jane, but they hold a God-given authority."

"But she purposely keeps things from me! And then tests me to see if I'll do what she says!"

"He who honors his parents shall live long upon the earth. Remember that, the fifth commandment?"

"I'm afraid that if I go down there, it'll kill me. I can sense a real darkness below our feet. She can't reassure me that it's safe down there when I'm this scared."

"Oh, I'll reassure you then," he said. "You'll be fine. God is with us always, even unto the ends of the earth, in the shadow of the valley of death."

"But people aren't always fine, though. Even though God is with them."

"Then it's just their time!" He sounded completely confident in his own theology. "And it's not your time to go down there yet. When that day comes, I know you'll descend with your head held high. You're brave, Jane. I can tell."

I rolled my eyes, but still, I hoped he was right.

9

WHEN I ARRIVED AT THE OSPREYS' HOUSE THE NEXT DAY, Derek was the one to greet me at the door. Mrs. Osprey was closed up in her bedroom, but she'd left me a list of things to do. A list! She had never missed the opportunity to order me around to my face. Mr. Osprey was out gathering firewood, and Derek's job that day was to supervise me, which galled me, since it probably meant I couldn't let Doll Mary do my work. Fortunately, Derek helped me complete the list. Various foods had to be cooked: loaves of bread, a cake, homemade noodles, and pesto sauce. This was in addition to filtering all the water and doing all the cleaning, including the bedpans. We talked as we worked.

"Why are you doing all this for my parents if you really don't want to?" he finally asked me.

"Grandma sent me here."

"You do everything she says?"

"Well, she never really told me what to do before all this happened. The Disaster, I mean. Before then, I studied what I wanted, did what I wanted, lived where I wanted."

"She loves you unconditionally?"

"Well, she doesn't respect all my decisions, but she still loves me, I think."

"Would she have loved you if you were like me?"

"You mean, if I killed someone? I don't know. Do your parents still love you?"

"Unfortunately," he said. "But that makes it even more complicated. I wish they'd forget about me."

"But you came all this way to be with them. You're doing what they want, just like I'm doing with my Grandma."

He smiled. "I didn't say I don't relate to you. I'm not sure why I'm doing this either, though. Why can't I just stay away?"

"It was easier when we had options," I said. "Now everything's changed."

We talked about the old days as we worked, recalling diversions like cosmic bowling, dramatic reality shows, celebrity gossip, hamburgers. Realizing we were only talking about low culture, we also said how much we missed art museums, classical music, public radio.

"Don't some radios work?" I asked.

"Even if they work, there's no signal."

"I know one family had a CB radio."

"Did you try to use it?"

"It broke, they said. And anyway, it's not mine. The funny thing is, since all that's happened, private property seems even more sacred than before. I used to take meals and drinks and all kinds of resources from other people without a second thought, but now it's all so precious. I have nothing but my labor to offer in return. Everything we have is stuff Grandma accumulated, supplies she got from a guy named Bill who used to live around here. I have no right to anything, really."

"So we're kids again, cut off from the world, depending on the resources of our guardians."

We were quiet for a while as we worked, me chopping basil into tiny bits, him mopping the kitchen floor. I wondered if Doll Mary was bored or glad of the break.

"There's one other thing Grandma has," I said. "A kind of magic."

"She always seemed like a witch to me," he said. "I used to think magic was evil. Then something strange happened."

"Oh?" I pictured Doll Mary curled up like a fetus in my backpack. Some strange things had happened to me as well.

"She moved to that house about five years after I killed my poor brother Vern—about fifteen years ago. She heard what I'd done, like I suppose most people did, and she took an interest in me, read me Bible verses."

"Really? I thought she didn't believe in that." I was the one who should have been reading Bible verses, but my Grandma, with all her pagan ways, had read the Bible to a poor kid who'd lost his brother. Well, who'd split his brother's head in two with an ax. Derek seemed so kind and thoughtful, though. I still felt sure that anything horrible he'd done really was merely due to some childish temporary insanity.

"She read me verses about the seasons. A time to do this, a time to do that. But also about cold and harvest and heat. She always emphasized the importance of nature and the seasons."

"Why did she read that to you, I wonder? She's never read the Bible to me," I said, feeling a little jealous.

"She saw I was haunted by my brother and needed spiritual help."

"Haunted?"

"His spirit was following me around."

"That's the magic you saw? A ghost?"

"Sort of," he said. "Your grandmother released him from me. She offered to keep him at her house, and since that day, I haven't seen him. Have you seen his ghost around your place?"

I'd experienced strange things there, of course, but I hadn't seen a ghost, so I told him no. "Not that I'm the most sensitive. I'm not like Grandma. Or even that kid Mary. She's said some weird things about the house, but I haven't noticed a ghost around. I wonder if he's...hiding somewhere." Of course, I thought about the cellar below the cellar, but that was a secret.

We were both tired when we parted ways, and I walked home alone that afternoon. On the way, I decided that Mary knew things she wasn't telling me.

When I got home, there was no fire in the chimney, no dinner cooking, no water boiling. Grandma was out, and Mary sat on the couch in a listless pose, thumbing through a picture book about anthropomorphic mice with Doll Laura at her side.

"Where's Grandma?" I said.

"Gathering stuff."

"You seem sad," I ventured.

She didn't answer.

"I have a question to ask you." I pulled Doll Mary out of my backpack and sat her beside Doll Laura, to show how close we were. "I've been talking to the Ospreys' son, and he told me about a little brother of his who died young. Have you seen any ghosts around here?"

Mary's eyes widened, but she kept quiet.

"You have! But why haven't I?" I believed in God, after all, so believing in ghosts wasn't such a stretch. I'd never really thought about ghosts, though.

"I don't know," Mary said.

She annoyed me sometimes, I admit, but especially at that moment. She was acting like a clever criminal who knew how to keep me in the dark. I got up to grab my doll and go to my room.

"Wait!" she said. "Grandma said I couldn't tell anyone about the things I've seen here. Even you. She made me promise. Can't we be friends, though? You never read to me anymore!"

I realized it was true, I hadn't been reading to her. Had I gotten too busy? No, it was something else. It was the doll. Since I'd been letting her wear my skin, I'd felt different.

"I've been working hard at the Ospreys," I said. "I got too tired. I'm sorry."

She rested her chubby face in her hands and smiled. "You gave your doll food and water."

I blushed a little. "Yes. I even borrowed your doll, which I guess you know."

Mary nodded. "Laura told me she went into your room. You were asking her a bunch of questions, too."

"She wouldn't answer. Everything's gone all upside down for me. I'm starting to feel scared of this house."

"It's always been scary," Mary said. "Even I know that, and I was only here a couple of times before my dad left me here."

"Maybe you're more sensitive than I am to certain things." It should have been obvious to me, but I only realized as I said it: Mary had some sort of gift that Grandma appreciated, and that was why she's living in our house. My mother had made the two dolls, but Mary got the smarter one that could talk. Mine only did boring chores.

"I don't like it here, but Grandma says I'll get used to it," Mary said, shutting her big brown eyes tight. "I miss my family."

"I'm so sorry, Mary. I'll talk to her for you. I had no idea you were depressed. You never told me."

I should have known, though. Of course a child taken from her family would be sad. Why hadn't I considered it? I would have noticed before, in my former life. At the library, strangers often approached me to help them with their problems, and I was happy to help. The new life in the woods, without conveniences, had made me so tired and confused. Or maybe it was the Ospreys. Or something about Grandma's house itself.

Rather than wait for Grandma to come back whenever, from wherever, I told Mary I was going out to search for her, but I'd leave Doll Mary with her and Doll Laura, I suppose so Doll Mary could protect them. I knew she was very strong. Mary was disappointed, but she picked up her picture book and waited in the light streaming in from the window. The days were shorter as we approached the equinox, so I figured I had an hour to search before the sun began to set.

Grandma had been making a garden in the backyard, which appeared paltry compared to the Ospreys' but had some promising-looking tendrils reaching out from the earth. I wished I could tend our garden instead of theirs, but apparently it was Grandma's domain. In one corner of the yard, she already had many herbs growing; and between the woods and garden, we had a field of weeds she sometimes picked over, but she wasn't in either of those locations. Where else would she go gathering? I went down to the creek to look for her there.

On the banks, I found some sweetroot, a plant I knew Grandma gathered for stomach troubles. I gathered some myself, using the hem of my shirt as a little basket. I did it unthinkingly, without intending to pause my search for Grandma.

She found me that way, when I was behaving just like her.

"Good job, Jane!" she said, and for some reason, the sound of her encouragement was more unpleasant to my ears than the sound of her scolding.

"Where have you been?"

"I have many things to do each day. Why were you looking for me?"

"I've learned some new information."

She invited me to sit on a tree stump, and sat on another one nearby.

While I spoke, I kept hold of the roots in my folded shirt. "Derek told me about his brother Vern," I said.

"Which one?"

"What do you mean?"

"He had two brothers named Vern." She gave me her mischievous little smile, and I was appalled by her morbid sense of humor. The Ospreys' terrible decision-making was nothing to laugh at, as far as I was concerned. I wasn't sure what to say to her, since the idea of two Verns put me in a bad mental state.

"Derek said Vern is a ghost, and that you offered to keep him at our house. Is that true?"

Grandma nodded. "*That* Vern is kept where you can't see him, so don't worry."

I was getting to a point where nothing surprised me, but her revelation that a ghost was living with us still made me mad. I wouldn't have ever stayed over at her house if I'd known it was haunted. "Mary said she's seen him."

"I've taken Mary to places in the house where you haven't been," she said. I couldn't tell if she was informing me or taunting me.

"She has some kind of special perception, right? Something I don't have."

"You could have it," she said. "Mary is more open-minded, though."

"She wants to go home, Grandma! She misses her family. It's not fair to steal her away to become a witch-in-training. We should try to track down where her family went, find that farm they mentioned. She needs them."

Grandma looked almost offended. I rarely managed to offend her, so I felt some combination of guilt and pride.

"Jane, I wonder about you sometimes. You're more like a child than she is. Don't you realize that her family is dead?"

It hadn't even occurred to me. "All of them?"

"She's so young, I couldn't tell her the truth, though she knows it anyway with that sense of hers. Her brothers died first, then her mother, then at last her father. He wished for death sooner, let me tell you. I tried to heal them, but I failed. I promise I did my best."

Grandma looked down and scuffed the dirt with the toe of her sandal. Another new emotion from her! Shame. I'd never seen it before.

"How did they die?"

"They didn't follow my instructions for how to filter their water. They thought they knew better than an old woman like me."

The base of my throat burned with pity, with grief. I hadn't given her family a second thought. If Grandma hadn't saved Mary, she'd have died, too. "Oh, Grandma."

"I have my agenda, Jane, but I don't want to see anyone suffer for it. I never have."

She'd always been charitable in her way. After all, she'd taken me in when my mother died. "But what is your agenda?"

That sparkle returned to her eye. "I'm trying to help you understand, but as smart as you are with books, you're slow with nature. If I could tell you outright what's happening and what needs to happen, I would have already done it. But you need to figure it out for yourself."

"It makes me hate you, though." Her rare burst of honesty that day made me feel I could be honest, too.

"At least you get to be unconscious sometimes. I never do. The horrors that hide in your dreams rule my daytimes. At any rate, we should be getting back to Mary before dark, don't you think?"

"Poor Mary!"

"Poor orphaned Mary."

We made our way home, and I was extra kind to Mary as Grandma made beans and instant mashed potatoes for dinner. We played with our dolls, and then I read her a chapter of another book about the dolls' namesakes, *Little House in the Big Woods*. We'd finished the prairie book, and it had left me feeling uneasy, but the *Big Woods* book was a prequel. That family was like us, making the best of things while staying in place. How admirable, in a way, to stay in one place. If only they had never left their woods, they wouldn't have faced so many troubles, so much poverty and violence and disease. They would have faced another set of problems, but all the while, they'd have been hidden and tended by the trees.

Maybe it wasn't so bad to live out in the middle of nowhere after all.

10

THE NEXT DAY, I WORKED WITH DEREK AGAIN INSTEAD OF using Doll Mary to do my chores. I wondered if she was growing restless. Then again, unless Grandma was using her in secret, she'd just been in a box from the time between my mother's death and my attaining the ripe age of thirty-three. Either way, I couldn't risk bringing her out while Derek was around. He was watching me closely; I suspected he was interested in some sort of romantic intrigue at the end of the world (or the world we knew). I wasn't interested in that, but I did need friends, so I tolerated his company. When he offered to walk me home that afternoon, I accepted, and this time, he agreed to go inside with me.

We found Grandma inside, crushing up some herbs while Mary watched. She was teaching her the trade! I felt jealous of their shared witchery, and I wondered if it was too late to prove myself.

"I think you know why I returned," Derek said to Grandma. "I want to see my brother again. I'm grateful you helped release me when I was a child, but even now the memories of him still haunt me. I can't go on unless I tell him I'm sorry."

"You didn't come to town to see your parents, who adore you? Who forgave your act of violence?" Grandma said, smirking as usual.

"Not really," he said.

That surprised me. Maybe Grandma was right that I didn't understand anything. If Grandma had freed him once from the ghost, why risk another haunting? What if the ghost took a liking to him again?

"I can take you, but it's dangerous," she said. "He's in the cellar below the cellar."

So that was her secret! Maybe that was why I'd always felt ill-at-ease about the place. There were ghosts down there.

"Can I come?" Mary said.

"I suppose so."

"What?" I said. "You can't take a child there."

"I've been there before!" Mary said.

I couldn't believe it. I was being replaced! "She's not even your grandchild!"

"I've offered to take you many times," Grandma reminded me. "You never wanted to."

"Because it's evil!"

"You just don't want to deal with the dirty work," Grandma said, waving her index finger like a Kindergarten teacher. "So you leave it to me, Rest assured, someone has to deal with it!"

I didn't see why anyone needed to deal with evil things. Then again, I wasn't going to voice my worries to Grandma anymore, as it was clear she'd only use them against me.

"I want to go, too," I said, surprising even myself.

Grandma knew better than to praise me or look happy

with my decision. After all those years of wheedling me, she simply nodded once, got a candle, and asked us to follow her downstairs.

We descended into the cellar, passed by its comforting supplies of cans and bottles, and stopped before a small bookshelf stacked with tubs of protein powder and drink mixes. Grandma pushed it aside to reveal a small door. I'd never been able to find it, because it wasn't hidden in the floor but in the wall. Grandma knocked on the door (to warn the ghost?), paused, and then opened it and led us into the passageway, holding her candle-flame out ahead of her. The doorway was just the right size for Mary to walk through, but the rest of us had to duck to pass through.

We followed her down a set of rickety wooden stairs and emerged into a small bunker, where a man I didn't recognize stood holding a lantern. I shrieked, and he shrieked, too.

"Calm down, Jane," Grandma scolded me.

I did, as he appeared harmless, tremulous and slender with pale puckered skin and a full head of icicle-colored hair.

"And you too, Bill." She stepped aside to make room for Derek. "Now, this is Vern's brother, and he wants to see him again."

"No kidding! The one who killed him, or the other one?"

"I'm the one who killed him, sad to say," Derek said, holding out his hand, which Bill gave a firm shake.

"So you're the Bill that Grandma's been talking about?" I said.

"Your grandmother generally doesn't permit lies, except in the service of keeping secrets," he said. "It'll be the death of me."

The space there underground was nicer and larger than you might expect. Someone (presumably Bill) had dug a sizable room, and secured the earth floor and walls with strips of wood. Cans and jars lined these walls, too.

"How did you know all this would happen? The Disaster?" I said. He gave me the impression of a friendly hobbit or gnome more than a paranoid apocalypse prepper.

"It was obvious! I mean, I catch some wavelengths when I meditate, but besides that, I read the news like everyone else. I got interested and did some research, and passed my info on to your Grandma."

"Yes," I said. "I'm grateful you cared so much about Grandma."

"I worry about everyone, but even more than that, I worry about someone being up there to care for what's below."

I didn't like the sound of that and wanted to know more, but Grandma interrupted.

"Anyway, this is Bill," she said, "as you've gathered. He's a secret, so don't go blabbing about him. Bill, this is my granddaughter Jane, and you've already met little Mary."

"Indeed," he said, setting the lantern on a small wooden table, which was covered with whittling tools and wood scraps.

"What's all this for?" I asked.

"Spoon-making," he said, with a hint of pride. "It's an old habit."

How many times had I slept over at her house while below me underground, a strange man carved spoons for no one? I wanted to slap him and Grandma for keeping such a creepy secret from me. "Are you going to explain why you are down here?" I snapped.

"Your Grandma and I are old friends, and we're in the same business," he said, maintaining the utmost politeness with me in spite of how I was treating him. "I'm here to help guard the place—mainly when things get dicey. I can reach my house by tunnel, so it's easy to come and go. You all are welcome to come over anytime! Just tell me, and I'll put the kettle on."

"Guard it from what?"

"Exactly," he said, and moved a small red carpet from the corner to reveal a trapdoor in the floor. "I guard the upper from the lower, and the lower from the upper. Never the two shall meet."

"I don't want to go down there," I said, even though Mary was standing by my side and looking up at me like I was her hero. She'd already been down there!

Bill, Grandma and Derek began talking among themselves, and I realized they intended to go down there.

"No one else has to go," Derek said. "I'm the one who murdered my brother, and I'm the one who has to go down there to make peace with him."

"You certainly can't go without me," Grandma said.

"I can go back down there," Mary said. "I'm going to be brave."

They all looked at me. How could I be the only one too afraid to go down there? I felt so ashamed.

"I guess I'll go," I said, though as they gathered around the trapdoor, I hung back behind them.

Bill said he had to stay above to guard, but whether for us or against us he didn't say. Maybe both.

The trapdoor opened up to total darkness, and again Grandma led the way, climbing down a steel ladder while still clutching her candle in one hand. I admired the athleticism she moved with, her ability to hold a candle while scrambling down a ladder with one prosthetic leg. I knew I couldn't accomplish a feat like that.

The ladder was long, and I was the last of us to hit the

hard ground. Grandma's candlelight flickered over the walls of the stone chamber, which was almost thc sizc of hcr living room. The cracks between the stones teemed with an odd beige moss that reminded me of neglected teeth, and the whole place smelled like a garbage can on a cold day, decaying but preserved just enough to keep it from pure rot. Grandma led us towards a crooked wooden door with a tarnished brass knob, and I reluctantly followed, hanging back a little.

"How is all this down here?" I said, but the others ignored me. They seemed to understand. Why was I the only odd one out?

Grandma opened the ugly door onto a pitch-black room and crossed the threshold, seeming to disappear even though she carried the light. The other two followed, each of them immediately consumed by the darkness and gone from sight.

I'd been to a haunted house once with my college roommates, and I'd cried and begged the actors not to hurt me. My roommates and I laughed about it later, but I never went to another event like that. This felt the same, watching the others disappear into a dreadful place. But it was too late to run away.

As I approached the doorway, there was a sense of being pulled towards it:, some strong force. Then I was all alone, in my own space, wandering in a land without a light. The ground was hard stone at first, but it grew softer. A pleasant flutter arose in my chest when I realized I wasn't afraid anymore. Not there, not even in the lonesome darkness.

"Hello?" I said, sensing some other beings were present. New ones.

I sensed they wanted me to sit, so I sank down to the comfortable ground. In the darkness, I felt a feather touch. Then another. Then another.

Soon, it was as if dozens of the smallest, loveliest birds

were fluttering their wings over my skin, the lightest brush of fingertips. A strong smell of resin enveloped me. Fresh and sweet. When I opened my eyes, it was no different than when they were shut. Feathers, fingertips, erosion, entropy. I submitted to everything.

I could have stayed there forever, but I didn't.

11
WHEN VERN SPOKE THROUGH ME

I ARRIVED RIDING A DARK HORSE OR DRIVING A BLACK CAR, and here I am. Here I find myself. I was riding a shadow, maybe. Hear me, brother? You disturbed my spirit by coming to see me. You made me leap out of my nest into this woman. She's the only one whose insides are spacious enough to take me.

I am fine. See? I am unraveling. I was until you bothered me. Since Mother Perch took me in, I've been undoing. Soon, or someday, or in half an eternity, I'll leak through the fissures of that place, and I'll be free.

An unbaptized child. That's what I was. Mother Perch took me in. Someday she might take you, Derek.

You were jealous and you killed me. You said it was the spirit of the Lord, or an angel. But you lied. Didn't you?

It wasn't like you. It shocked us. You were a sensitive child, and you hated blood. Even now, you seem uncommonly kind. Not the sort to have committed that kind of crime. I will hear you out.

After I died, I followed you because I was trying to understand. Why did you really do it? I accused you of lying so many times because I wanted to see if you flinched.

Mother Perch brought me here where her friends could wash away my worries, wash away my imaginary flesh. There are others in there with me, and more to come. Mother Perch gives us to her friends down there to be unraveled. Until I can be just spirit. I have been here, being worked on. Waiting. I had hoped never to see you again. Now I know how much flesh is left in me.

You were my best friend. We played together every day. Oh, brother. I thought you loved me. I'll listen to your story. Confess your sins to me. Give me your reasons. I hope to forgive.

12

Anyway, I was half asleep when it happened, when Vern used my mouth to speak. I didn't know how he'd gotten inside me, but I could sort of hear him, though his voice sounded muffled. I felt sorry for him, but I wished he'd go away. I wished Derek would go away, too. Over the sound of Vern's murmurs, I could hear Derek crying and apologizing. I had no idea if the brothers were happy with their meeting, whether it was helping them both.

Then a light shone on me, and someone roughly grabbed my arms, and I tried to hit them but missed. Grandma shouted, and I was dragged away. When I glanced back at the lovely place I'd left, I thought I saw many pearls.

Vern was gone, and I was left alone in my body, except Derek was holding my hand and crying. I snatched it away. Disturbing and disgusting stuff. I wanted nothing more to do with it. For some reason, he had possessed me. Briefly. Why me? I could ask that about a lot of things. I have, and I get no answer. There's no point in it.

When I tried to stand up, I got dizzy, but Bill caught me before I hit the ground again and made me sit down at his table. He handed me a can of pineapple juice and told me to drink up. He said channeling was rough on the blood sugar. Grandma, Mary, and Derek were looking down at me like I was a freak, but at least I had Bill. I wondered if he was my Grandma's lover, or if they were just friends. He was a strange-looking man, his bare feet covered with dirt and his hair unkempt. Short and hunched over. I thought it possible he was another species altogether. Still, I felt a kinship with him.

"I didn't give permission for that to happen. Let the record show," I said, and Grandma gave me that stupid twinkly-eyed grin of hers.

"If you go down there, to the cellar below the cellar, you never know what will happen," she said. "Haven't I told you that for a long time? There are many spirits there, and once they're receiving the Treatment, they don't like to be disturbed."

"You told me to go down there!" I said. "You kept pressuring me."

"It's part of your birthright," she said. "Or at least, I think it is. If you never descend, you'll never know."

"I wish I didn't know about any of this stuff. I wish I was dead." It probably sounded childish, and I shouldn't have said it in front of Mary, but I felt so disgusted with myself. Now I knew it was possible to be something other than myself, to have someone else's voice speak through me. I didn't like it, and I hadn't given my permission!

Without further discussion, I got up and went out the little door, leaving them all in Bill's secret chamber.

Once I was back in my bedroom with the door shut for

privacy, I fed Doll Mary and gave her something to drink. She stood up and looked at me expectantly, but I wasn't even sure what I wanted her to do. I just didn't want to be alone, maybe, even though I'd isolated myself. I wanted a more comforting presence than the others in the house, and Doll Mary was the closest thing I had to a mother.

"What do I do now?" I said.

She stood there, waiting. Something about her reminded me of my mother, though of course they looked nothing alike. My mother wasn't blue. Her features weren't made of glue and yarn. It was something about the way the doll swayed when she was standing. Or maybe it was the way she seemed to see through me.

"I wish I knew what to do with myself. Should I go back to the city? Do I stay here forever? Should I build my own house, one without a cellar?"

Doll Mary didn't answer, of course, but something about the slanted blue of her eyebrows on her flat face made her seem sympathetic. She tucked me into bed, and I fell asleep. It was the soundest sleep of my life.

I woke the next morning to find Doll Mary sitting next to me, upright and unsupported. In her mitten-shaped cloth hands, she held a cigarette, unlit. I hadn't smoked a cigarette in over a decade, but I took it from her and hid it behind a book on the bookshelf in the guest room. I had no doubt that Doll Mary had ventured out in the night and brought me back the cigarette as a souvenir, like the dove brought an olive branch to Noah after the flood.

I felt rested, in spite of all my psychic travels, and I remembered my dreams so clearly. I was walking along in the darkness, tripping over trash now and again. I went through a dark apartment that reminded me of the one I'd shared with Bea and Penny before the Disaster. All in disarray. The smell!

It was just another place to be, another place where it was hard to survive. I felt so alone there, as alone as I felt at home. That is, at Grandma's home. I'd never had a real home. Maybe it was time.

When I arrived at the Ospreys that day, Derek opened the door for me again, but this time I didn't make eye-contact with him and asked to work alone. I avoided him all day, and he might have been avoiding me as well. It was hard to say. I didn't want to know what he was thinking. Seeing him the way I'd seen him yesterday made me hate him a little. He'd told me he killed his brother, but I hadn't known what that meant until I was present in the moment with him and his ghost brother. I'd never even had siblings, much less murdered one. Lots of things are acceptable when theoretical.

Doll Mary did my work that day while I went down into the water, or whatever happened when she took over my flesh. I was afraid it wouldn't be as lovely as before to descend into the water, to shake off my body for a while. It was like my body had been invaded when Vern took it over. So even though I'd always loved my time away from myself, the sweetness of the water and slime and mud and absence of boundaries, I felt too angry to enjoy it. I began to feel boxed in by the experience, like I couldn't catch my breath.

When I came to, I was gasping for air by the side of the creek, and all three of the Ospreys were looking down at me. Doll Mary was slumped on the ground beside the creek.

"He told us you were a medium for Vern," Mrs. Osprey said without any salutation. "Please let us hear from him!"

"Calm down," Mr. Osprey muttered to his wife. "It might be witchery."

"I don't care. I want Vern back."

She crouched on the ground beside me, muddying the knees of her nice gray slacks.

"I need to talk to him. I have something to say to him. Please, hon. Please." She'd never been so gentle with me. But then, she'd never truly needed me before.

If I could have blinked my eyes and destroyed the whole forest, turned it to whiteness and darkness, I would have. That was not what I had the power to do, though, fortunately. Instead, I collected Doll Mary and all my anger and told the Ospreys to follow me.

The three of them lagged several steps behind me on the road back to Grandma's. At one point, Mr. Osprey jogged to catch up with me, but I turned around and sort of snarled, and he let me be. The trees were lovely that day, though the air was humid and still. They waved their little leaves when they could, offering me their greenness.

I barged right in and told Grandma what we were going to do. Down down down, to the cellar below the cellar, to conjure up the murdered boy again. This time, Mary was too scared to go, and Mr. Osprey (though he wouldn't admit it) was too. Derek claimed he'd said all he had to say to his brother and made his peace, so he was staying behind as well. I felt a victory over all three of them. All had tried to take something from me, in different ways. I shouldn't have hated them the same way, but I did. Mary was a cute girl, a little too smart, but sweet enough. I had no reason to hate her. Sometimes in the most unspeakable hours of the night, a hidden part of me wished she'd died with the rest of her family. Whenever that thought snuck in, I'd wake up horrified.

"I'll lead the way," I said, taking Grandma's candle. I led them down into the cellar, through the tiny door, and down the rickety wooden stairs to Bill's chamber. I looked for him, but he wasn't around. His absence was a blow.

"He told you he comes and goes," Grandma said.

I carried on to the trapdoor. As I took the ladder down to the cellar below the cellar, I tried to balance the candle, but it fell to the ground and snuffed out. Nonetheless, I carried on. Once I reached the tunnel, I felt my way along the stone walls, trying to find the ugly wooden door. Grandma lit another candle and caught up to me, bringing light just as I felt the rough wood.

"This time, we'll do it my way!" I said. In retrospect, I have to admit, I must have shouted.

"All right, all right," Grandma said. "Go ahead, do it your way! Why would I try to stop you?"

I stood in front of the door, but before I opened it, I shouted something I can't quite remember. Something like, "Come here, Vern, but this time I'm in charge!" Something stupid like that, something you don't need to say to a spirit or even a partial spirit. Vern knew why I was there.

This time when the door opened, I didn't get sucked in. I didn't go to the comfortable place where I felt feather touches brushing against my skin. I remained on the cold floor of the infernal cellar and let Vern inside. I listened to him, and I relayed the information, but I didn't let him take over my lips or eyes.

"I'm sorry for dying, Mother," Vern said and I said.

Mrs. Osprey took me in her arms as if I were her son. La Pietà.

"I'm sorry for all my mistakes as a mother," she said. "I'm sorry we showed Derek you were our favorite. If we hadn't, he might not have..."

"You aren't my mother anymore," Vern said. "You have no reason to apologize."

This led to too much wailing, and I warned Vern not to make his old mother so upset. I didn't want to deal with it.

"It's okay, Mother, I forgive you," Vern said. "I've moved

on. Mother Perch is my mother now, until I'm set free by the Unraveling."

"Don't move on! Stay with me!"

"I have to. I can't stay in one place forever! When you die, do you want me left behind? Do you want to stay behind to cry for me? Mother, before I came to this place, I was collecting your tears. I kept them in a cup. When I came here, I poured the cup out as an offering to the Hands who do the Unraveling. I set your tears free. I want to be free as well."

"I have no idea what you're talking about!" Mrs. Osprey cried out, and I was afraid she was going to have a heart attack.

I told Vern to be less opaque. A ghost should know how to be clear.

"There's a lot of life that still clings to us when we die," Vern said. "I was an unbaptized child. Not because I hadn't been put in water by a preacher. No, but because I'd been exposed to so much evil. It clings to me like an invisible sheet, but the Hands will brush it away."

"I'm so sorry we didn't baptize you! We had no idea you'd die so young!" Mrs. Osprey said, cradling my face and Vern's face.

"I'm glad it's like this. Mother Perch helps all unbaptized children. There are many of us in the Unraveling Place. It's a good place. I promise."

She still didn't understand, kept asking him to stay, apologizing. I said whatever Vern said, but I chose to say it. If he'd said something I thought was wrong, I wouldn't have relayed it.

"I have to go back," he said at last. "You don't know what these excursions cost me. Please don't bother me again."

"But what is happening to you down here?"

"I'm being separated. Like you separate the silt from the water when you drink from the creek.

"Have to boil it for a long time, too, and run it through a filter," Grandma said, like she really cared about the proper technique. We all ignored her.

Vern explained it another way, and I understood at last. "Some folks are taking care of me, separating me. Their many skeleton hands brush all my skin away. It sounds worse than it is. It's nice, really, and soon I'll be free."

So there were many hands down there. Those featherlight bony fingertips. They were doing the separating. Where did the hands come from? Even then, after all I'd seen and done, I didn't want to know.

"I love you, and I want you to be at peace," Mrs. Osprey said at last.

"Then let me surrender to this work. Goodbye, Mother."

With that, he was gone, his soul slipped back inside the door. Over her shoulder, I caught a glimpse of many bonewhite fingers reaching out to catch her son. I suppose they had to finish whatever process was happening.

The conversation turned Mrs. Osprey into a mess, like a rag all wrung-out. We helped her out of the darkness, then up the ladder, up the stairs. Grandma, unflappable as always, said she'd escort the three Ospreys back to their place.

I found myself alone with Mary, needing to be a caretaker for her when I was still vulnerable, shaking with the aftermath of rage and the spirit's imposition. I wanted to offer her some dinner, but instead I sat on the couch and stared into the fire, trying to snap myself awake.

"Sleep if you want to," she said. "Grandma will be back soon."

"No, no. I can stay awake. It was just so strange. What did you see when you went down there?"

Mary shook her head. "I don't want to say. I was looking for my family."

"Did you find them?"

Instead of answering, she put her thumb in her mouth.

"Well, it must be an awful place. I hate to think it's there underneath our feet."

She removed her thumb and smoothed out the little pinafore Grandma had made for her.

"It's like what happened to Mary and Laura. The real ones," she said. "They were so scared on the prairie. There were dangers everywhere, and then mosquitos. Remember?"

"I remember. The mosquitos made them sick."

"They almost died."

Mary burst into tears, so I sat next to her and gave her a one-armed hug. I felt truly sorry for her, but I didn't know how to comfort kids. Or anyone else.

"We're not going to die anytime soon," I said.

She looked surprised. "How do you know?"

"Maybe Vern told me. Somehow, I know more than I knew before."

"There are too many things to know down there. I'm scared, Jane."

She cried some more, and I continued with my lackluster hug.

"You don't have to do anything you don't want to do," I said, but that only made her cry harder. We both knew that wasn't true.

When Grandma returned, she teased us for being so mournful and serious.

"What's gotten into you, Little Mary?"

"I'm scared!" Mary said. "I don't like it down there."

"No need to fret," Grandma said. "You two might visit, but that place is my domain. As long as I'm kicking, it's mine.

When I eventually, on a day far from now, run out of lifetime, then maybe one of you can inherit your own little dream kingdom."

"What will the other of us do?" I said, some of my anger returning. I was her granddaughter. It was my birthright, even if I didn't want it.

"Whatever she wants," Grandma said.

But I was starting to want strange things.

13

When I went to the Ospreys the next morning, feeling more than a little bashful about our intimacies of the day before, Derek's old white truck was missing. I knocked on the door, and it swung open on its own. Their living room was dark, and empty of most of their belongings.

They had moved on.

"Blessed miracle," I said aloud. I walked throughout the house and garden to make sure there was no trace of them, but they'd taken everything they could, it seemed.

Once I was confident they were really gone, and that they hadn't salted the earth on their way out (in fact, they'd left a few ripening vegetables for us to pick), I ran to get Stephanie and her boys. I wanted to share the glorious moment, and Grandma and Mary seemed too far away.

Stephanie wasn't as happy as I was, though. She cried for their absence.

"We've lost so many people," she said as she followed me to the Ospreys' old house.

Her boys were excited, though, buzzing along ahead of us both. Like me, they'd had to work for the Ospreys.

Once we were back at the house, they ran all over, scouting out the treasures left behind and gathering them for me and Stephanie. We sat on the Ospreys' comfortable couch and let them gather goods. Vegetables, of course. Figs. Cans of corn and peas and beans. Cans of tuna fish and sausage. Medicine kits. They'd left a lot behind, but it was clear they'd taken all they could. Clothes, food, seedlings, pills, firestarters, all piled up in the back of that truck. Good for them!

"It's our garden now," I told Stephanie. She'd recently bathed and smelled pleasant enough, like the creek, but she looked wan and tired. Dark circles under her eyes. "We'll have pumpkins soon."

"Oh," she said. That was all.

"Mom, we can live here!" her son Andrew told her.

"That's a good idea!" I said. "I hadn't thought of that. There's more space here, and so many supplies."

All three of us, the boys and I, watched Stephanie to seek her approval. She gave a curt nod, and that was enough for us. We celebrated.

Then I remembered our chores. We still had to do them. That is, we had to attend to the garden and filter the water. It was a small load of work, enjoyable in its way since I was no longer feeling the weight of the Ospreys' watchful eyes, so I didn't need Doll Mary. The boys went down to the creek with water jugs while I weeded and admired the garden, which was already cycling away from summer vegetables and into true fall. It had always been my favorite time. Cold air, woodsmoke, spices. Halloween. I forgot, for a moment, our troubles. How we had no electric heat.

My daydreams were interrupted by shouts from the boys.

They'd found something bad at the creek. I told Stephanie to stay put and ran to the boys, but she trailed behind me.

Beside the creek lay a body, sprawled facedown in the grass. Stephanie told the boys to stay back and helped me turn the already stiff body over. Derek was no longer handsome now that the life had left his face. I cried out to him, but he couldn't hear. I hadn't forgiven him for what he did to his brother, but I'd intended to. Now it was too late.

"Gunshot wound," Stephanie said. "In the back of his head." She said it like a detective on television.

We looked around for a gun but couldn't find one.

"They shot him execution-style," she said. "Their own son."

Tears filled my eyes. How could they? Because they loved him less than Vern?

So they hadn't abandoned their house just for the sake of getting out of town; they were fleeing their crime. But like Derek, they'd carry it with them wherever they went. I believed they'd be back one day to seek out Derek's forgiveness, just as he had returned for Vern.

It occurred to me that they hadn't simply left him to rot. They'd known we'd find him. And he was unbaptized, wasn't he? He was really just a child. His parents must have hoped we'd give him the same treatment as Vern, down below the below.

"I know what we have to do with the body," I said quietly, as Stephanie shed her own tears.

"I can get the boys to dig a hole," she said. The boys were standing there staring at us with their mouths hanging open. It was a shame to spoil their innocence, but there was no way around it. We were such close neighbors now, we even had to handle each other's dead.

"No, we have to take him to those hands in the cellar

below the cellar at Grandma's house. They'll take care of his body there, in the Unraveling Place."

Stephanie looked at me like I'd lost my mind, but she must have trusted that Grandma would know what to do, because after I got the Ospreys' wheelbarrow, she helped me load Derek's body into it.

We wheeled him down the road to Grandma's house, and the boys took turns with me, pushing him along. All three of us were worried about Stephanie, who looked rather frail, but she kept saying she was fine.

"God in heaven!" Grandma said when she saw what we carried.

"We think his parents shot him," I said, though Grandma hadn't asked what had happened to him. She just nodded, seeming so unsurprised that I wondered if she'd known what the Ospreys were going to do before they did. Or maybe she'd been there, hiding behind a tree near the creek, watching the execution, Maybe she was somehow everywhere.

"Well, you know what we have to do!" she said.

"I hope they'll be happy together again at last," I said. It was a wonderful place for the dead down there, and I hoped Derek's spirit would feel something like happiness there.

With marvelous lightness and strength, like an ant, Grandma crouched beside the wheelbarrow and lifted Derek's lifeless body like it was a child's. I had no idea how she possessed such strength, but then again, she'd hidden much of her magic from me all along.

I rushed to grab a candle, and she carried the body down the stairs to the basement, then through the small doorway to Bill's room (again he was absent). She dropped the body through the trapdoor, and it thumped onto the hard ground of the cellar below the cellar. He felt no pain, though. With both hands now free, she descended to attend the body, and I followed her. She laid him out on the cold stone floor. He looked peaceful in the light of Grandma's candle.

"You finally understand me now, Jane. You have to freeze yourself to the ground like roots in the winter to be as strong as I am, to carry what I carry. You never know when you'll need to carry the dead. They don't die on your schedule. I'll be very busy this winter, and you'll have to take charge of this place. Someday Mary will be old enough if you want to switch out with her, but for now, it's all on you. Do you want to practice?"

"Practice what?"

"Guiding him in there. Giving him to the hands."

I shuddered with fear for the first time in a long time. "What do you mean?"

"Quit stalling!" Grandma had always been so impatient. "Just tell me. Can you do it yourself?"

I certainly didn't want to. I was used to Grandma taking care of the most unpleasant things. "What do I do?"

"Open the door. Carry him in there. Hand him over. Come back. Simple!"

If I stopped to think too much about it, I knew I'd never agree. Without another glance at Grandma, I opened the door into loamy darkness and felt such wonder and peace, like I was coming into an air-conditioned building on a sweltering day. I crouched and tried to lift Derek like I'd seen Grandma do, and found he was light as a doll. Whatever magic Grandma had with the dead, I had it too.

I wouldn't have chosen this kind of magic if I could have chosen for myself, but then, no one had asked me what I wanted to do.

I carried him over the threshold like he was my bride, and Grandma shut the door behind us without another word.

Merciless as always! I hoped she wasn't just tricking me, killing me like the Ospreys had killed their own.

"Hello?" I said, hoping for someone to come along. It was uncanny staring with open eyes into the darkness, and trusting it.

As I stepped away from the door, the stony ground became soft ground again. Like spongy moss. The darkness seemed to change shape and shade, from square to elliptical, from black to darkest gray.

"God, I'm walking through the shadow of death," I said. "Please help me get through all this."

The gray lightened into red, then pink. All it illuminated was a maze of stone walls, but it was like the sun had risen, blessing me and the dead with sunrise. Where was the light coming from? Above my head, in the stone ceiling, I saw little openings that let in light. From where, though? It was none of my business. My business was to carry the body. And I did, until I felt something familiar, that featherweight against my back.

"It's you," I said to the hands. I carried on past a stone wall and turned the corner to find curtains—dark curtains that kept out the light from certain areas. Without pausing to ask, I pulled one back. There was darkness there that the light couldn't touch, darkness heavier than curtains. From inside that darkness, the skeleton hands reached out. Those featherlight fingertips. The touch of hands sans flesh. The touch of articulate bone.

The hands turned up to me, showed me their palms (such as they were). I could see they were my friends, offering to bear my burden. I carried Derek one last step, and they took over. Gently, gently, they bore him away behind the curtain, then into the darkness. I knew what they would do because I'd felt it in a dream, when I was briefly Vern. Those bony hands were going to brush him for ages, whittling away the flesh over time, over time, over time. Eventually, the body would be bone, the soul split, and the spirit would escape, up through those skylights. To where? None of my business. My only business was to bear the weight of the bodies downward, to hand them over. The hands of death's valley would bear the bodies and bare the bodies.

The place was awful and beautiful, and it made me feel a little hope. I said goodbye to the hands (there were so many curtains, there must have been a thousand bone hands), and I ran back to the darkness, the stone, and through the door to Grandma.

She was smiling when I reached her, but it wasn't an ironic grin this time. For possibly the first time in my life, I saw her show real pride in me.

"You did it! I was sure you'd come screaming back. You fought me so long about going to that place."

"It's beautiful in there." I wanted to explain how I felt about the place, but I couldn't find the words. It was better than anything, and the opposite of everything I'd ever feared. I'd been so wrong about the cellar below the cellar for so many years.

"That's a good thing, Jane, because no one else can see its beauty. Even Mary was very scared. But she's so young, and she'd only wandered in there without me to look for her family. She has some seventh sense, you know. She knew without knowing that her family was dead, and that I'd taken their bodies there. Once I found her down there, I let her look around, but she couldn't handle peering behind the curtains. Did you see what was there?"

"I looked behind a curtain and saw skeleton hands and moss," I said. "But I know there's more."

"There's always more in there," she said, wistful as a young lover.

"Is Mom there?"

She shook her head. "Gone. Mercifully. Her flesh is gone. Spirit mostly gone. All but the little part she left behind in those two dolls. That was her blessing to us."

I thought one day I might return to check on Mom, to make sure she'd moved on. Maybe one day I'd peel back all those curtains and see what was there. See Derek again, maybe, when he was only partially skinned. There was time for that later, though, I hoped. I was in no mood to return today. Still, it was like my heart had lost a layer of skin down there. It had peeled away like an old sunburn, and a new layer had been revealed.

We climbed up the ladder to find Bill there waiting for us, sitting at his little table and carving at a spoon.

"Another body?" he said.

"Derek," Grandma said. "It seems his parents shot him, then skipped town. That's the best we can figure out."

Bill shook his head. "Bad business. I'm glad his parents aren't down there. It'd be a lot to ask of me to guard them. I have a feeling they'd wake up from their death, get right to their feet, and climb up here to bother me. Some people are so demanding."

You couldn't barter with death, even if you had the best garden around. Death probably didn't care about vegetables.

"What happened to that green pepper?" I said, suddenly wondering if the hands were involved somehow. "Did the hands take it? Did they reach into the world and take it out of my hands?"

"Why would they do that?" Grandma said.

"Maybe they're hungry for a vegetarian meal," I said, and Bill laughed.

"Maybe they wanted to teach me a lesson."

That was a guess, but Grandma and Bill just looked at each other. I still had it wrong somehow.

"Maybe they wanted to lure me somewhere," I said.

At last, Grandma smiled. Bill only sighed.

"There's no escaping them," he said. "That's for sure. Even if you don't take the bait right away."

A sobering thought. Maybe the choice to descend wasn't even mine. I might have belonged to the underground no matter what I did.

"Too much pondering for one day," Grandma said, and we went back upstairs to reassure Stephanie, Andrew, Charles, and Mary that Derek was at peace now.

"And we should be, too!" Grandma said. "It's almost time to eat." That was all she said about it, but they all seemed relieved. They knew that the problem of the dead body was no longer theirs.

Grandma made us all a big lunch while the kids ran around outside, playing tag. The boys were careful not to knock Mary down. They were good boys, and I told Stephanie I thought so.

"Yes, I'm grateful for them," she said. "I hate that all this happened, but it will be nice to move. Our house doesn't have a fireplace, and it's already getting chilly at night."

"That house is well-insulated. We can all stay there when it snows," Grandma said, returning us to practicalities.

It felt good to think about planning for winter, about the wood to be chopped, the vegetables to be preserved, the snow we could melt to drink. My heart had turned to winter, like a brute I was falling in love with.

⁂ 14 ⁂

I WOKE UP IN THE MIDDLE OF THE NIGHT WITH A SHADOW standing over me. I wanted to scream, but I was paralyzed. A guttural sound came out instead, like I was trying to say a German word.

"Oh, sorry," the figure said. He lit the candle on my bedside table, and I saw it was the only Bill from downstairs. It was unsettling to see him in the upper world.

I sat up in bed and held my pillow to my stomach as if it were a shield. "Are you here to murder me or something?" I asked him, shivering with sweat.

"Of course not!" Bill sat in the chair beside my bed. "I needed to speak with you in private, that's all. Not in front of your Grandma. Hard to pull one over on her, but she happens to be out of the house now."

"Where does she go at night?" I said. There were so many questions I wanted to ask about her, but I wasn't sure if it was treasonous to take secrets from Bill. Maybe he was her lover, after all.

"Oh, different places. It wouldn't make much sense to you. She picks up the slack that other people leave behind."

"She told me she was gathering. Herbs and the like."

"I'm sure that's true, too. Anyway, we'd better make it quick, because who knows when she'll return. She's smart as the devil." His eyes twinkled in the candlelight, reminding me of Grandma's perpetual look of irony.

"What is it?" I said.

"I just wanted to remind you of the importance of compassion. Your Grandma hardly has any, but you're different from her. You aren't as gifted, so you have to be different."

Harsh words! But I listened.

"Weren't you and Derek friends?" he asked. "But you don't take the time to mourn for him? All these people have died around you. Your civilization is sort of dying, too. Don't you care? You seem like you don't."

He looked really concerned. Surely he wasn't human, but I couldn't figure out what he was.

"Don't worry about that," I said. "I've done so much mourning lately, but I've had to stuff it down."

"It's my business to worry about whatever crosses sides. You are someone who passes between this world and that one. I have to guard both places."

I felt more certain than ever, though, that there was nothing to worry about. The hands were helping Derek, giving him help he'd never received in life.

"I don't know what it means to have responsibility for that place, not yet. Give me some time to get used to it, then remind me about compassion," I said.

"There's never as much time as we need to figure things out. After all this time, I'm still confused by so many things. And I miss the old country sometimes. If I can get someone there to take over my work here, maybe I'll return one day."

"Oh, to Switzerland?"

"To the Alps," he said. "Where I was born and raised."

"Like Grandma?" I asked, but he wouldn't elaborate.

"Your Grandma says I talk too much."

"We aren't even supposed to be here in this country," I said.

"No kidding. Some insisted on coming here, and they spread out. Then I was asked to come look after them. Now look at the state of this land! And I'm so far from home!"

"Me too," I said. Still, I wondered if I could make Grandma's house my home one day.

"But in the meantime, you want me to have more compassion? Why?"

"So you don't make the same mistakes your Grandma made when she took over. She was too tough on the dead at first. She judged them too harshly, and it doesn't help. It doesn't help for us to judge. Whatever happens down there below my feet, I know it gets rid of all the need for judgment."

He stood up to leave and shook my hand.

"I have more questions," I said.

"Your Grandma would kill me if she knew I'd told you this much. She's a big believer in learning on the job."

He left me pondering his words, and struggling to fall back sleep.

THE NEXT MORNING, as I was reading to Mary and Grandma was cleaning up from dinner, we heard a knock at the door. Our friend Dan was back again with another wheelbarrow full of demon jars. I helped him move them this time without any fear of the basement. It was almost cozy to me now, the layers of the house. The living layer, the storing layer, Bill's room, and then the hands' home.

"You're in a good mood!" Dan said.

"Grandma says I don't have to go to help with the garden anymore. She says Stephanie's kids can handle it, and I have too much work to do here."

"Do you really hate gardening so much? I think it would be fun."

"You can help them then!"

"Sure, when I'm in town." He winked at me. "Turns out I'm a rolling stone."

Once we were done, we joined Grandma back upstairs. "What's on the agenda for today?" Dan asked her.

"I have a great job for all of us!" She clapped her hands, and I knew we were in trouble. "Today we're going to clear out Mary's family's old house. We'll leave Mary at Stephanie's, and we'll pick up some useful stuff."

What could we say? She was right, it was time to see if there was anything we could scavenge, especially anything of Mary's to make her more comfortable or help her remember her family in a positive way.

As we walked along the road, Grandma and Mary lagged behind. In a whisper, Dan said to me, "Your Grandma says that you've seen the place we can put all these jars. To make them safe."

"Oh." I imagined the skeleton hands carving away at the glass until the demons were free. Free to go where? Through the fissures in the ceiling of the place. After that, it was God's business. "Yes, I know of a place."

"She said you'd help, but that you might be stubborn about it, because you do the opposite of what everyone wants you to. I know that's true, since we dated, so I wanted to make sure. You promise you'll get rid of these jars for me?"

"We only went on three dates!" I said. "When was I stubborn with you?"

"I could tell you thought I was stupid to begin with, and then when I showed you my jars, you pretended like you were fine with them but you refused to even try to understand them, no matter how well I explained them to you. You just didn't get me. Those jars are the whole purpose of my life! That's what you laugh at when you laugh at the jars."

Compassion! Could I muster any? "I'm sorry," I lied, hoping I'd be sorry later.

"Have you been reading your Bible and praying more?" he said. "You seem nicer now."

"No, I've been too busy with all the stupid chores we have to do now that we don't have power. I'm definitely not nicer now. I'm less nice. But probably more honest."

"You seem nicer," he said, which made me feel a little better about myself. Bill had certainly caused me to feel some self-doubt, though I'd pushed it down.

We dropped Mary off with Stephanie along the way.

"It's turning cool!" Stephanie said, cheerful as always.

"Thank God," I said. "We can move on from this horrible summer."

"We can move on," Stephanie said. "But I don't know if things will be less horrible."

I couldn't help but feel things were looking up.

Mary cried as we left. She knew where we were going, no doubt. I couldn't imagine what she might be feeling.

When we arrived at her old house, we found it to be relatively neat. Grandma had indeed disposed of the bodies (carrying them alone to the cellar below the cellar) and cleaned up the mess. There was a chilling emptiness, though, a sense of being utterly alone, once we stepped through their doorway.

"You don't really need our help, do you? If you could drag those bodies around, you're strong enough for most things," I said. "So what are we doing here?"

"My strength comes when lifting the dead, but nothing else. At any rate, we can't have ugly unclaimed territory like this," Grandma said. "We have to decide what to keep and what to leave. Then we ought to burn their private things we don't take. Their furniture, knick-knacks, mementos."

Dan and I both objected to the burning plan. What if we needed the materials? We were scavengers on the face of the earth. We needed all the spare wood and towels and anything else we could get.

"Fine, it'll all be up to you soon enough," she said in a prophetic sort of tone that made me nervous. "Gather what you want or need from here, as long as it isn't tainted with sorrow. That's why we're here, to scavenge!"

I waded into the ugly atmosphere of the house, from room to room. I remembered how cute Mary was with her brothers when they were playing together in the yard. I wished we could take them out of the cellar below the cellar, just for a minute, so they could play once more again. In what once was Mary's room, I looked at her plastic dolls. I picked one up and thought of her. Dolls, stuffed bears, little trinkets. They had an equal likelihood of making Mary happy or sad. They might unite her with the tragedy of the past, or with whatever happy memories were left. Behind me, Grandma entered the room and put her little hand on my shoulder.

"Was she happy here?" I asked Grandma.

"Do I look like I'm psychic?" Grandma said.

I turned around and saw that twinkle in her eye again. "I guess not," I said. "Do you think she'd like these things?"

"Don't really know. What if you take one toy for her to test it out?"

I took an ordinary-looking teddy bear with light-brown fur with a red bow tie. Like any other bear you might find, but it had been hers.

"I want to show you something," Grandma said, and she took me to the stairs that led down to the basement.

"I've done enough following you into cellars," I said, but she ignored me, and I followed anyway.

The family had some supplies down there, like boxes of laundry detergent and packs of paper towels. Nothing necessary, but all useful.

"Do you want me to carry this stuff upstairs?" I said.

"We'll let Dan do that," she said, and led me through a side door.

I braced myself for something weird, like another cellar beneath a cellar, but I was relieved to find an ordinary little office. On the desk, there was a small device with a handheld speaker attached.

"A CB radio," she said. "It belonged to Mary's father, but it had a loose wire. I fixed it up and gave it a listen or two myself."

I sat at the desk with Grandma behind me. I had the sense she was supervising me. I turned the knob on, and then adjusted the dial to listen out for people talking. It was silent on many channels, but a few had voices. One channel had people laughing. Laughing! I couldn't stand that for some reason, not while sitting in the house of a dead family. So I went on by. On one channel, someone was giving instructions. I listened in a little longer and found it was about how to close up a surgical incision. I didn't want to think about that either, so I kept going. I kept flipping around and around, surveying my fellow men and their quaint new world problems. On one channel, some people were talking about how to set up medical clinics. Someone else was talking about using the vehicles they had to rescue old people who lived alone and take them back to some campsite.

It was clear to me that some people had established larger communities, what you might call compounds. Not just a handful of people like what we had, but communities of over a hundred. They were out there organizing, trying to solve problems.

I thought about pushing the button to speak, to break into a conversation to let them know we were out here. Maybe we could go join them, be part of something bigger, lend a hand to a larger band of humanity instead of just a few folks. Make a difference. Start over again?

"Shouldn't we let them know we're here?" I said to Grandma.

"What do you think?" she said.

I realized I was doing what I often did, which was to seek her advice instead of deciding myself. I wasn't just stalling for time. I wanted her to be responsible for the decision.

It was time for me to take some stance on my own behalf. There were benefits to staying in a small group for the time being. We probably had a bigger batch of food saved up than most people did. It seemed wrong to hoard it, though.

"The obvious answer is to contact these people, to have some kind of larger community looking out for us," I said. "Things are going to get harder and harder, maybe."

"True."

"But there's no rush, I guess. The thing is...there is something we have to protect. The cellar below the cellar. If the wrong people get into it, they could ruin it. It's not something everyone would understand."

"We've been in such a small circle, a little cocoon. We

managed to rope Dan in pretty easily, which is no surprise when you consider how crazy he is. But most people won't understand the cellar below."

Not everyone we met out there would be as crazy as we all were. It would take time and patience to find the right ones. In the meantime, we couldn't abandon the cellar below the cellar. Too much important work was happening down there. Who knew how many beings would pass through there in the coming years?

I turned the radio off and faced her. "Grandma, what is that place? Did you know about it before you moved to that house? Was that why you moved here? And how long have you known Bill? Whose hands are those skeleton hands?"

When I was done asking all that, I wanted to cry. It felt like I was poisoning myself by asking. And yet, I was getting older, and didn't I deserve to know? That weird place was also mine.

"It would kill you to hear all I know at once. I learned the truth about that place over time, and it's taken me more than a lifetime to work it out. For now, what if you just ask one question? Then learn the rest yourself."

I thought about what I wanted to know most of all. Maybe there was a key, one question that could answer all the rest. If I knew who Bill really was, maybe that would tell me something about the cellar below the cellar—or maybe he had to learn about it just like me. I could ask what the cellar below the cellar is, but she might just say it's a hole in the ground! She loved tricks like that. There was one thing, though, that might change everything else. Or it might not.

"If I want to, can I move away and leave the cellar below the cellar to you and Mary?"

"Now that's a smart question!" Grandma looked almost

proud of me for the first time I could remember. "The answer is, you can do anything you want."

"But it will have consequences," I said. "If you die or disappear and I'm not there, maybe things won't work down there anymore. Or maybe they'll be just fine."

"And the truth is, I don't know. Not even Bill knows, I don't think. What matters more is if you care. If you care about that underground place. If you feel you want some part in it."

It was the kind of question I wasn't sure if I could answer even if I had infinite time to think about it.

"Are you two done down there?" Dan called down the stairs. "I loaded up the wheelbarrow already!"

I took Mary's teddy bear upstairs, and Grandma took a box of laundry detergent. We inspected what Dan chose, and Grandma put some stuff back that she thought would remind Mary too much of the past. Then we set out on our way, leaving the place to its awful emptiness.

When we arrived back at Stephanie's new house, Mary accepted the teddy bear without a word, but she put her thumb in her mouth. I took that as an uncertain sign. I wished we had a child psychologist with us, but we didn't even have any books about raising children. She didn't seem curious otherwise about her old house or the contents of the wagon. At least, she didn't ask anything about it.

"I told Mary she could have a sleepover here," Stephanie said. "She said she's kind of scared of your house. Is that all right?

"I suppose," Grandma said. "Any natural child would be scared. I just wasn't sure if Mary was natural like that. I'm still not sure."

To my surprise, Grandma was letting her stay with

Stephanie without a fight. It seemed she let her go without a second thought. For a time, at least.

We left her there, and as we walked home, I was also surprised that I felt sentimental about it. Mary was pulling away from us and drifting towards Stephanie's maternal energy. I knew Grandma's house wasn't a place for a child to live, and I was relieved in one sense, but maybe I'd miss her after all. Still, I couldn't see me or Grandma filling in as Mary's parents. She needed someone nurturing, like Stephanie. Maybe someday she would grow up and take my place, become the keeper of the cellar below the cellar. She was gifted, after all. Probably more gifted than I was. For the time being, though, I had work to do. I had to carry the dead who belonged down there. Whenever Mary wanted to visit me and the dead, she was welcome anytime.

That night Grandma opened a bottle of red wine, and she and Dan and I all drank while she made spaghetti.

"What's going to happen when this runs out?" Dan said. "How will Catholics have communions?"

"They'll figure out how to make more." Grandma said. "I'm going to learn how to make wine, but I'll have to make it with muscadines and honey."

"Will you teach me?" I said.

She promised she would. I wondered what else she'd teach me, what other secrets I still had to discover about this new world. Maybe Dan would stick around and she could teach him about the cellar below the cellar too. He was a pastor, after all, another kind of usher between worlds. Maybe he could go out gathering at night and do whatever else she did, and I could be like Bill, standing guard.

Once Dan was tipsy enough, he gathered the courage to ask what he'd been wondering about. "When do I let go of all my jars?" he said. "I don't want to press my luck."

"When the time is right," Grandma said. And that was that. There was nothing more for him to ask.

Whenever that time was, I knew I had something of my own to cast into the cellar below the cellar. My Doll Mary. If some part of Mom was still in her, she needed to be set free. I prayed Mary would do it, too, would let go of Doll Laura when she was grown. It's easy to get too attached to a talisman, but they aren't supposed to last forever.

15

DAN CAME AND WENT WITH HIS WHEELBARROW ALL autumn, and Grandma always found a place for his jars. We started calling him Wheelbarrow Dan instead of Pastor Dan, which fit him better. Mary stayed with us some nights, but mostly she stayed at Stephanie's house, just as I'd expected. I spent a lot of time there, too, helping teach the kids whatever I remembered from my schooling. I didn't know what would matter to them anymore, but I didn't try to guess. There was no way to predict it all.

We had parties sometimes, taking turns hosting. Stephanie had one on Halloween, and she made little streamers out of construction paper. She said she'd be keeping them for party after party, that it was a good investment.

We had a harvest of so many pumpkins that we had enough for carving. Each one of us got our own, except Mary, who worked with Stephanie since she was too young to hold a knife.

Grandma carved a portrait of me, though it wasn't very good. It looked more like Mr. Magoo than me, but she admired it when she was through. "My granddaughter, the beautiful spinster."

I was flattered by her praise, and I took spinster as a compliment by then. I carved an outline of a human skull, which was maybe too on the nose. I wasn't considering the recent dead, though. I was sorry for Derek and Mary's family, but there was nothing I could do. Or rather, I'd already done all I could do. I didn't even think of the big house as being the Ospreys' anymore. I thought of it as Stephanie's, as if it had always been hers. Most of all, I was thinking about the underground below our cellar, of all those skeleton hands. Did they belong to skeleton bodies? Were those bodies attached to skulls? Since I didn't know, and I knew better than to go down there just to expose them, I had to play around with the idea. I think my carved skull looked good. I'd even say it was lifelike.

Andrew carved Spiderman. He'd traced an image from a comic book to make it, and it was the best of all. Charles carved his own face, and I admired his self-regard. Stephanie, at Mary's direction, carved Mary's mother as best she could remember her. They hadn't known each other well. That was a depressing part of the night, but we acted like it was nice.

Grandma and I carried our glowing pumpkins home, and while she left hers outside, I took mine down to see if Bill was in his room below our house, to see if he might like it. I had that place on my mind, I guess.

He was there, and he appreciated my handiwork. "Funny damned tradition," he said.

"Does giving a gift mean I have compassion?" I said.

"Not if you give it to me. I'm like your pet down here. Maybe if you give it to your enemy."

"All my friends and enemies could be dead."

He shrugged. "If you want to be dramatic. I really do

appreciate this gift, though. I'll enjoy it this evening, carving my spoons and reading by a pumpkin's candlelight."

He had a ratty old coverless paperback on the table, and I resolved to give him some nice books from upstairs to read for Christmas. The *Little House* books. *Lost Horizon.* I didn't know what his tastes were, but he seemed to have a lot of downtime.

"You never truly answer my questions, but can you tell me one thing? Where do all those spoons you make go?"

"I give them to the skeletons," he said. "If you want to know what they do with them, you'll have to ask them yourself someday."

One cold morning in mid-December, I woke up in the frosty air to find that the house felt different somehow. Everything was colder than usual, but it also felt freer. I wrapped one of my blankets around my shoulders and went to the kitchen for breakfast, and there I found a note left on the kitchen counter.

It said: *Dear Jane, I love you so. This is a beautiful time, but I can't share it with you because I have to work. I have to help other people in their time of trial. Winter can be a trial for many, especially now. While I'm gone, please watch the house. All my Love, Grandma*

"How annoying!" I said. Now I'd have to do all the chores myself. Then again, we wouldn't have to filter water from the creek as long as it was snowing, and snow was already piling outside the door, and it was easy enough to cook for myself, and for Bill when he was around. I could go to Stephanie's anytime, too, since we shared everything.

I brought in the pans I'd set out overnight, and I let the

snow inside melt. I'd need to collect much more to warm for taking a bath.

All day, I worked around the house, taking breaks to eat bread and fig preserves. At night, a new solar storm was blazing, though I hadn't heard any loud noises to accompany it. Soft and undulating, like green and red scarves hanging down from the stars. After dinner, I read an anthology of nature poems by that aurora light, utterly at peace. I was worried I'd be scared alone or miss Grandma and Mary, but I didn't miss anyone or anything. I was happy just to read by the cold green light.

I went to see Bill the next day to ask if he knew where Grandma was and when she'd be back.

"Winter makes her young and strong," he said. Everything he said was mysterious, after all. "She has to use it."

"But am I really ready to do this while she's away, to take her place here?"

"Certainly!" he said. "You're a natural down there. You can channel spirits. The hands seem to welcome you, to regard you as one of their own. It's a curious thing."

"Why?"

"I don't know what makes one person suited for one thing, and another suited for another. I wish I knew."

So did I! I felt my affinity for the underground afterlife was lucky and unlucky at the same time. It wasn't exactly a paradise, but then, it was necessary.

All of us missed Grandma, but Stephanie and I had fun with the kids, playing board games and making snow forts. We weren't quite as attentive to our chores as we were when Grandma was present, but we got most things done. I even had extra time to read, and to write about what had happened to me.

Dan returned on Christmas Day, wrapped up in multiple

coats he'd scavenged along the way. We'd last seen him in November, when the leaves were all dead on the ground, for our harvest party—we didn't want it to be Thanksgiving since that seemed so stupid to us, but we called it a Feast Day. On that visit, Dan had asked us all what we wanted for Christmas and took notes, promising to be back before then. Grandma had said she wanted for nothing, but I asked for as many books as he could bring.

His presents were hidden under a tarp on his wheelbarrow, and I was glad to see goods from town. He was so cold, though, I took a bottle of whiskey from the cellar and warmed it on the fire with some water and spices.

"I knew you'd be back in time!" I said. "Like Saint Nicholas. The kids will be so happy."

"I got them some interesting toys," he said. "And I went by your library for a pile of books for you. Want to see them now?"

I did, refusing to wait for the proper time to open my presents. He'd gathered wonderful hardbacks of classics like *Great Expectations*, *Sula*, *Madame Bovary*, *A Touch of Mistletoe*, *Lolly Willowes*, *Remains of the Day*, and others I'd wanted to read but hadn't gotten around to yet.

"I'll get more when I go back after all the snow has passed."

"When you go for more demon jars?"

"I got the last of those in November." He looked sheepish. "But I like traveling, and I like bringing stuff to people, carting it around."

I'd made paper dolls for Mary (who said she preferred dolls to teddy bears, as long as the dolls were grown-ups), and I planned to gift Grandma's old paint set to Andrew, and her cornhole set to Charles. I had prepared some homemade mead to give to Stephanie and Bill, but I'd forgotten all about

Dan, since I didn't see him often. "Is there anything you'd like for Christmas? I meant to ask before, but I can get started on it now."

"Just one thing. We need to talk about those jars."

I sighed. Him and his jars. He never stopped thinking about them.

"I mean it," he said. "See, I thought that someday I would understand the demons if I kept collecting them. I'd ask them why they had so much lust for blood and suffering, and they'd whisper back, saying they were lonely or scared or that they'd been bullied or that they were just plumb crazy. But it hasn't worked. I don't think it can work up here. Maybe only down there, in that place below. Meanwhile, if someone ever let them out of the jars, who knows how much pain and suffering they'd cause?"

"You're giving up on your experiment?" The idea made me a little sad. We'd lost so much recently.

"It's time to let them go. I'll never understand them, and they need to be transformed. Maybe God can talk it over with their spirits and make sense of it. Maybe down there, the evil parts of them can learn to be separate from the rest. That's what your Grandma seemed to want."

If I got rid of the jars, it would be my Christmas gift to her as well. Wherever she was.

I agreed to his proposal. We called down to Bill, and he came up and helped carry all the jars back down the stairs and down the ladder, to pile them up in front of the ugly old door that led to the room of unraveling hands.

While we carried our glass armfuls, careful not to drop any, Bill told us about the renovations he was making to his house and how we'd finally have to visit in the spring. Something to look forward to.

At the last minute, to my surprise, Dan held back one jar

to keep on the cellar shelf with the bullets and hydrogen peroxide. His special Ted Bundy demon.

"There'll never be another like it," he said. "I know that should make me get rid of it sooner, but I... Maybe if I try harder with this one, I can really come to terms with it. Really understand how it got to be with the way it is."

I'd lived long enough with a basement full of demons in jars that I wasn't afraid. I said he could keep it there for the time being.

While we were letting things go, I got something of my own to sacrifice. My gift from Mom, Doll Mary. I would gift it back to Mom, whatever portion of her remained within the ugly blue doll. As Grandma had once said, spirits weren't meant to be trapped forever.

When the time came, I reassured Bill and Dan that I could do the rest myself, and they climbed up the rickety stairs, saying to call out if I needed help.

Armful by armful, I took the jars and ventured into the darkness. I felt for soft bones and set the jars beside them or in their grasp. What fun to have such mysterious and awful creatures as friends, ready to help me. It took a while to transport all of the jars, and the time I spent in the dark space made me feel a bit weepy. Somewhere in the shadows, my mother and Vern and Derek and Mary's family were all on their way to freedom. And others I didn't know about, and still others yet to come.

I held the blue ragdoll in my arms, and I said, "Goodbye, Doll Mary. Goodbye, Mom." I baptized her rough face with tears as I thanked her, as I told her I wished I knew her better. Someday I'd throw Doll Laura in too, but Mary still needed her. Doll Laura was a talisman fit for these dark ages, which had been luckier than I'd expected them to be. For me, anyway. Not for the Ospreys. Not for Mary's family. All I could do was pray that no demons found their way upstairs and under the rickety door. Bill was there to guard, of course. Old Bill.

I could already hear the sound of bones gently scraping glass, and I was pleased. They'd do their work.

After I was done, we all drank mead together. The men were in a jolly mood, not understanding my feelings about relinquishing the last gift, the last blessing of my mother, so I acted merry, too.

TO CELEBRATE CHRISTMAS, we delivered Dan's presents to Stephanie's house, where we found an egg-and-onion breakfast casserole waiting for us along with biscuits and frosted cakes.

"Where did you get these eggs?" I asked, surprised she'd made friends with the same locals the Ospreys claimed to know.

She shrugged. "They just appeared in the cupboard."

Better to accept a gift than question it. We had all learned that. The eggs tasted good, and so did the rest of the feast. We were all so happy together. One big, strange family.

Over the last weeks, the others had begun to look to me for guidance on certain matters, such as herbal remedies, death and dying, and the afterlife. I knew very little about those things, yet I knew mountains more than they did. I had to use what wisdom I had to help my friends while they waited for Grandma to return.

After everyone went to sleep that night, I walked outside and searched the skies. Luminous auroras shone through the wispy clouds in waves of soft green with tinges of scarlet, like the sky had knitted us a blanket, and for the first time I truly understood that the lights were beautiful.

"But where are you, Grandma?" I asked. The biting breeze hit my cheek like a scold. "Are you coming back home?"

The wind answered, rustling the leaves, telling me that Grandma had other homes across the worlds, where souls followed her until she found them a place for their unraveling. Shadowed pine trees waved at me, and the sky undulated with shades of green that should not exist. I wasn't scared, though. Not anymore. I knew that I had to look after the lost in this world.

And now I knew the truth. I heard Grandma's voice as clear as if the cold winds were telephone wires. She'd spoken to me and only me. She was gone forever, and her house (and everything above and below it) was mine to tend.

I wished she could see how brave I was now. I stood under the green sky and cried for her, but I was also happy. I lived somewhere beautiful, with another beautiful place below, and above it all, a magnificent sky, rippling with bright colors.

ACKNOWLEDGMENTS

Many thanks to many!

Many thanks to my husband Justin for being my first reader for every project.

Many thanks to my parents Stephen and Carol, my brothers Sam and Ben, other family members such as Vivian and Hugh, and friends from various corners of life and the internet. Also, Bilbo.

Many thanks to my grandmothers, Catherine and Maxine. Many thanks to Marissa van Uden for joining me on this creative journey and editing her heart into this, and to everyone at Violet Lichen and Apex Books.

Many thanks to all tale-tellers, including those who gave us Vasilisa and Frau Perchta.

ABOUT THE AUTHOR

Ivy Grimes is originally from Birmingham, Alabama and currently lives in Virginia. She has an MFA from the University of Alabama. Her stories have appeared in *The Baffler, Vastarien, hex, Maudlin House, ergot., Potomac Review,* and elsewhere. She is the author of the collection *Glass Stories* (Grimscribe Press) and *The Ghosts of Blaubart Mansion* (Cemetery Gates). To learn more, please visit www.ivyivyivyivy.com.

instagram.com/grimivys

DON'T WAIT! *SCAN THE CODE* AND FEED YOUR IMAGINATION!

ABOUT VIOLET LICHEN

Founded in 2024, Violet Lichen Books is the sister imprint of Apex Book Company. Violent Lichen was created by Marissa van Uden to give a home to those dark, literary, weird books that might be a little outside of the norm. The imprint focuses on speculative ecofiction, Weird and New Weird, and moody science fiction with uniquely memorable characters.

Find out more at www.violetlichen.com.